DEAR DURWOOD

JEFF BOND

For my father.

Dear Mr. Oak Jones:

I am Carol Bridges, mayor of Chickasaw, Texas. We are located in the western part of the state, Big Bend Country if you know it. I thank you in advance for considering my injustice.

Chickasaw is the home of Hogan Consolidated, a family-run manufacturer of industrial parts. Hogan employs 70 percent of able-bodied adults in Chickasaw, and its philanthropy has sustained the town for ninety years. It's due to the Hogan family we have an arts center and a turf field for youth football.

Recently, East Coast lawyers and investment bankers have taken aim at the company. Multimillion-dollar claims have been filed, accusing Hogan of putting out defective parts. It's rumored the company will be acquired or liquidated outright. Massive layoffs are feared.

My constituents work hard, Mr. Jones. They have mortgages and children to feed. I have tried to find answers about the Hogan family's intentions, to see whether I or the town can do anything to influence the course of events. Jay Hogan, the current CEO, does not return my phone calls— and is seen dining at sushi restaurants in El Paso (eighty-five miles away) more often than in Chickasaw. I have gotten the runaround from our state and federal representatives. I believe it's their fundraising season.

As mayor, I have a duty to explore every possible solution to the challenges we face. I do not read *Soldier of Fortune* regularly, but my deputy police chief showed me your ad soliciting "injustices in need of attention." I feel certain injustice is being done to Chickasaw, though I can't as yet name its perpetrator and exact nature.

Alonso (our deputy chief) knows you by reputation, and assures me these details won't trouble you.

Thanks sincerely for your time,
   Carol Bridges
   Mayor of Chickasaw, Texas

Durwood got to the Chickasaw letter halfway through the sorghum field. He was flipping through the stack from the mailbox, passing between sweet-smelling stalks. Leaves brushed his blue jeans. Dust coated his boots. He scanned for clumps of johnsongrass as he read, picking what he saw. The first five letters he'd tucked into his back pocket.

The Chickasaw letter he considered longer. Steel-colored eyes moved left to right. He forgot about the johnsongrass. An ugliness started in his gut.

Lawyers.

He put the letter in his front pocket, then read the rest of the stack. The magazine forwarded him a bundle every month. In September, he'd only gotten three. At Christmastime, it seemed like he got thirty or forty. Folks felt cheated around the holidays.

Today, he read about two brothers who didn't steal a car. About a principal who got fired for being too aggressive fighting drugs in his school. About a bum call in the Oregon

State Little League championship twenty years ago. About a furnace warranty that wasn't worth the paper it was printed on.

Durwood chuckled at the Oregon letter. This one had been writing in for years. Maybe he figured Durwood didn't read them, figured some screener only put a couple through each go-round and one of these days his would sneak through.

But Durwood did read them. Every last one.

He put the letter about the principal in his front pocket with the Chickasaw letter.

Off his right side, Sue-Ann whimpered. Durwood turned to find the bluetick coonhound pointing the south fence line.

"I see," Durwood said of the white-tailed doe nosing around the spruces. "Left my gun back at the house, though."

Sue-Ann kept her point. Her bad hip quivered from the effort. Old as she was, she still got fired up about game.

Durwood released her with a gesture. "What do you say to some bluegill tonight instead? See what Crole's up to."

Durwood called Crole from the house. Crole, his fishing buddy who lived on the adjacent sixty acres, said he was good for a dozen casts. They agreed to meet at the river dividing their properties. Durwood had a shorter walk and used the extra time to clean his M9 semiautomatic.

Leaving, he noticed the red maple that shaded the house was leafing out slow. He examined the trunk and found a pattern of fine holes encircling the bark.

That yellow-bellied sapsucker.

Durwood wondered if the holes were related to the tree's poor vigor.

Out by the river, Crole limped up with his jug of moonshine, vile stuff he made from Jolly Ranchers.

They fished.

Sue-Ann lay in the mud, snoring, her stiff coat bristling against Durwood's boot. The afternoon stretched out, a dozen casts becoming two dozen. Then three. In the distance, the hazy West Virginia sky rolled through the Smokies. Mosquitoes weren't too bad, just a nip here and there at the collar.

Durwood thought about Chickasaw, Texas. He thought about East Coast lawyers. About the hardworking men and women who'd elected Carol Bridges to be mayor and stick up for them.

He thought about that CEO picking up raw fish with chopsticks in El Paso.

He thought, too, about the principal who'd been fired for doing right.

Crole said, "Got some letters today?"

Durwood said he had.

Crole grinned, showing his top teeth—just two, both nearly black. "Still running that ad in *Soldier of Fortune*?"

Durwood lowered the brim of his hat against the sun. "Don't cost much."

"They give a military discount?"

Durwood raised a shoulder. He'd been discharged from the marines a decade ago. He didn't accept handouts for his service.

Crole nodded to the bulge in his pocket—the letters. "Anything interesting?"

"Sure," Durwood said. "Plenty."

They fished into twilight. Durwood caught just five bluegills. Crole, twenty years his senior and luckier with fish, reeled in a dozen, plus a decent-size channel cat despite using the wrong bait. The men strung their catches on a chain. The chain rippled in the cool, clear water.

The Chickasaw job appealed to Durwood. The opportunity to fight crooked lawyers, to do something about these Wall Street outfits that made their buck slicing up American companies, putting craftsmen out of work until every last doodad was made in some knockoff plant in China.

Still, Durwood had trouble imagining the case. What would he do, flip through documents? Sit across a folding table from men in suits and ask questions?

Then he thought about the principal. About those gangs the letter had mentioned, how you could look out the windows of the dang school and see drug dealers on street corners. Intimidators. Armed thugs.

Durwood had an easy time imagining that case.

The sky had just gotten its first purple tinge when Durwood lost his bait a third time running.

"These fish." He held his empty hook out of the water, shaking his head.

Crole said, "There's catfish down there older than you."

"Smarter too," Durwood said.

Still, the five bluegills would be enough for him and Sue-Ann. Durwood unclipped the fishes' cheeks from the chain and dropped them in a bucket.

Back at the house, Durwood spotted the yellow-bellied sapsucker climbing the red maple. Not only was he pecking the tree, the ornery creature kept pulling twigs from the gray squirrels' nest, the one they'd built with care and sheltered in the last four winters.

"Git down!" Durwood called.

The sapsucker zipped away to other antics.

Inside, Durwood scaled and beheaded the bluegills. Then he fried them in grease and cornmeal. Sue-Ann ate only half a fish.

Durwood moved the crispy tail under her nose. "Another bite?"

The dog sneezed, rattly in her chest.

Durwood rinsed his dishes and switched on a desktop computer. He looked up Chickasaw. There was plenty of information online. Population, land area. Nearly every mention of the town made reference to Hogan Consolidated. It looked like Hogan Consolidated *was* Chickasaw, Texas, and vice versa.

On the official municipal website, he found a picture of Carol Bridges. She wore a hard hat, smiling among construction workers.

Handsome woman. Warm, lively eyes.

Next, Durwood looked up the fired principal. The man lived and worked in Upstate New York. For a few weeks, his case had been all over the local news there. A city councilman believed he'd been railroaded. Nineteen years, he'd served the school district without prior incident. The only blemish Durwood found was a college DUI.

Durwood hadn't started with computers until his thirties. His calloused fingers regularly struck the keys wrong, but he managed. This one he'd gotten from the Walmart in Barboursville, forty-nine bucks on Black Friday. It had its uses. A tool like any other.

"Well?" he said aloud, even though Sue was out on the porch. "Looks like a toss-up."

Durwood changed computer windows to look again at Carol Bridges. Then changed back to the principal.

At the bottom of the news story about the principal, he

noticed a bubble with *47 comments* inside. He knew people who spouted off online were unreliable and often foolish. He clicked anyway.

Good riddance, got what he deserved!

TOTAL RACIST WINDBAG, glad they fired him.

Durwood read all forty-seven comments. Some defended the man, but most were negative.

It was impossible to know how much was legitimate. Durwood left judging to Him, and Him alone.

But Durwood did know that the petitioner, the one who'd written the letter to *Soldier of Fortune*, was the principal himself. Not some third party. Not an objective observer.

What had seemed like a case of obvious bureaucratic overreach suddenly looked less obvious.

Now Sue-Ann loped in from the porch. Appalachian air followed her inside, nice as perfume. Sue settled at Durwood's feet, wheezing, rheumy eyes aimed up at her master.

He said, "What do you say, girl. Up for seeing the Lone Star State?"

The dog sat up straight, responding to the action in his voice. The effort made her mew. That hip.

Durwood laid his thumb down the ridge of the dog's skull. He felt pained himself, thinking of documents, folding tables, and men in suits.

CHAPTER TWO

It was a healthy drive, nearly two thousand miles, to see this Carol Bridges. Doubts remained in Durwood's mind. Petitioners he met through the *Soldier of Fortune* ad fell through sometimes. It would turn out their letter was misleading or flat false. Other times, the injustice had taken care of itself by the time Durwood arrived.

Once he'd driven clear to Nebraska to help a man whose pride and joy, a 1917 Ford Bucket T he'd restored from salvage by hand, had been denied roadworthiness by some city councilman with a grudge. When Durwood knocked on his door and asked about the hot rod, the man said, "The Ford? Guy made me an offer, I sold her a few weeks back."

Durwood decided it was worth the trip to hear Carol Bridges out. If he didn't like what she said, he'd tip his hat, get back in the Vanagon, and drive home.

Crole observed, "You could call."

Durwood was humping supplies into the van. "Folks can say anything on the phone."

The older man looked to the horizon, where the sun

would rise soon. His pajamas dragged the dirt, and he held his jug by two fingers. "They can say anything to your face too."

Durwood whistled to Sue-Ann.

"It's different," he said as the dog climbed in. "Lay off that shine, hm?"

Crole looked down at his jug as though surprised by its presence.

He answered, "Don't kill anyone you don't have to."

With a wave, Durwood took out. The van wheezed over mountain switchbacks and chugged steadily along interstates. By afternoon, Sue was wincing on the bare metal floor. Durwood bought her a mat the next time he stopped for gas.

They reached Chickasaw the following morning. Crossing the city limit, they saw fields of wheat and corn, and grain elevators, and dry, dusty homesteads. Factories burped smoke farther on. Billboards shilled for some dentist, somebody else who wanted to be sheriff.

Downtown Chickasaw was a grid, eight blocks square. Durwood saw the turf field mentioned in the letter and smiled. A boarded-up building with a sign reading, *Lyles Community Outreach Center*. A fancy hotel that looked out of place.

Next door to city hall, Durwood's destination, was a coffee shop called Peaceful Beans. The logo showed the name written along the stems of the peace sign. The light bulbs inside had those squiggly vintage filaments.

Durwood knew that these towns, rural or not, had all types. You got your vegan yoga instructors living next to redneck truckers—sometimes married to each other.

City hall itself was a stone structure two stories high. A

sign indicated the municipal jail was located in the basement.

Durwood parked. His bones creaked as he stepped from the van and stretched.

The woman working reception cooed at Sue, who'd rolled over on her back. The big ham. Durwood stated their business, declared his M9, and passed through a metal detector before being shown to the mayor's office.

Carol Bridges stood from her desk with a humble smile. "Mr. Oak Jones, thank you for traveling all this way for our town."

"You're welcome," he said. "Call me Durwood, please."

She said she would and handed him a business card with her personal number circled. Durwood placed the card in his blue jeans pocket. The mayor gestured to an armchair whose upholstery had worn thin. Durwood, removing his hat, sat.

"My dog goes where I go, generally," he explained. "She can sit outside if need be."

"Don't be silly." The mayor reached into a drawer of her desk for a biscuit. "If I'd known, I'd have brought in my German shepherd."

She didn't just toss the biscuit at Sue, as some will. Carol Bridges commanded the dog to sit first.

Sue sat.

The mayor squatted and offered the treat, palm up, her knees pinching below a dark skirt. Sue wolfed it down.

Durwood said, "We saw the factories on the way in. How many employees?"

"Forty-four hundred on the floors themselves," she said. "Plus another eight thousand in support roles."

"And it's all going away? Vamoose?"

Carol Bridges crossed one leg over the other. "That's how the winds are blowing."

She expanded upon what the letter had said. For the better part of a century, Hogan Consolidated had produced parts for various household products. Brackets. Pot handles. Stepladder hinges. Nothing sexy, Carol Bridges said, but quality components that filled a need higher up the supply chain.

Five or six years back, Wall Street began taking an interest in the company. They believed Hogan was under-leveraged and growing too slowly.

Durwood stopped her. "What does 'underleveraged' mean?"

"As I understand"—the mayor fluffed her dark-red hair dubiously—"it means you aren't taking enough risks. Your balance sheet is too conservative."

"Too conservative?"

"Right. You're not expanding into new markets. You're not inventing new products."

Durwood rolled her words around his head. "Suppose you're good at what you do, and that's it."

Carol Bridges looked out her window toward a pair of smokestacks. "Not good enough for Wall Street."

Thoughts of finance or economics usually gave Durwood a headache, but he made himself consider the particulars of the case now.

"But Hogan's a family-owned company," he said. "Can't they tell Wall Street to go to hell? Pardon my French."

"They were family owned up until 1972, when they sold out."

Durwood sat up in his chair, recalling her letter.

She seemed to read his thoughts. "They're a family-*run*

company. The CEO's always been a Hogan, but the equity is publicly traded."

"Hm." Durwood's head wasn't aching, but it didn't feel quite right either. "I read your letter different."

"I apologize, I didn't mean to be unclear." The mayor took a step out from behind her desk. "I hope you don't feel I brought you here on false pretenses."

They looked at each other. The woman's face tipped sympathetically and flushed, her eyes wide with concern. On the wall behind her hung the Iraq Campaign Medal and the striped ribbon indicating combat action.

"It's fine," Durwood said. "And they're facing lawsuits, you said?"

"Correct," the mayor said. "A class-action suit has been filed by customers claiming injury as a result of faulty Hogan parts."

"What happened?"

"A woman in New Jersey's toaster exploded. They've got two people in California saying a bad Hogan hinge caused them to fall. One broke her wrist."

"Her wrist."

Carol Bridges nodded.

"Falling off a stepladder?"

She nodded again.

"What're the Hogans doing?" Durwood asked. "They have a strategy to stomp out this nonsense?"

"No idea. I hear, just scuttlebutt from the cafe, that the company's going bankrupt." The mayor flung out an arm. "Somebody else says they're selling out to a private equity firm—one of these outfits that buys distressed companies for peanuts and parts 'em out, auctions off the assets and fires all the workers."

Durwood leaned over the thighs of his blue jeans. "You mentioned the CEO in your letter. Eats sushi."

The woman smiled. "Jay Hogan, yes. He's only twenty-eight, and I don't think he likes living in Chickasaw much. He went to college at Dartmouth."

"Whereabouts is that?"

"Dartmouth?"

Durwood nodded. He'd once met an arms supplier in Dortmund, Germany, the time he and Quaid Rafferty had stopped a band of disgruntled sausage vendors from bombing ten soccer stadiums simultaneously. He'd never heard of Dartmouth.

Carol Bridges said, "New Hampshire."

"If he doesn't like the place," Durwood said, "why didn't he stay east? Work a city job?"

She crossed her legs again. "I doubt he could get one. Around here, he was a screwup. They got him for drunk driving regularly. I was with the prosecutor's office back then. The police winched him out of the same gully four different times in his dad's Hummer."

"Why'd they pick him for CEO?"

"He's an only child. When the father had his stroke, Jay was next in line. Only pitcher left in the bullpen."

Durwood drew in a long breath. "Now the fate of the whole town rests on his shoulders. Fella couldn't keep a five-thousand-pound vehicle on the road."

Carol Bridges nodded.

Durwood felt comfortable talking to this woman. As comfortable as he'd felt with a woman since Maybelle, his wife and soulmate, had passed in Tikrit. Carol Bridges didn't embellish. She didn't say one thing but mean another—leaving aside the misunderstanding over "family run," which might well have been Durwood's fault.

Still, comfort didn't make a case.

"I sympathize, Miss Bridges," Durwood said. "I do. But I'm a simple man. The sort of business I'm trained for is combat. Apprehending suspects. Pursuing retribution that can't be pursued within the confines of the law. This situation calls for expertise I don't have."

He'd delivered bad news, but Carol Bridges didn't seem upset. She was smiling again.

"I have to disagree," she said.

"You need somebody knows their way around corporate law. Knows how to—"

"You're not a simple man. There's a lot up there"—her warm eyes rose to his head—"that doesn't translate into words."

Durwood held her gaze a moment. Then he looked down to Sue-Ann.

The dog was sleeping.

He said, "America is changing. For better or worse. A town like Chickasaw doesn't get the better end of it, I understand. There's injustice in that. But it's not the sort I can stop."

"Of course. I wouldn't dream of suggesting you can deliver us back to the 1970s."

Carol Bridges laced her fingers over her hair. A funny thing was happening with her mouth. Was she chewing gum? No, that wasn't it. Using her tongue to work a piece of food out from between her teeth? Durwood didn't think so either.

She was smirking.

"All I'm asking," she said, "on behalf of my town, is

this: Talk to Jay Hogan. Get a straight answer out of him. I can't, I've tried. The rest of the Hogans live in Vail or Tuscany. We need somebody who can cut through the bull and find out the truth."

Durwood repeated, "The truth."

"Yes. If the jobs are going away, if I need to retrain my citizenry to..." She searched around her desktop for some example—pencils, folders, a stapler. "Heck, answer customer service calls? I will. But we want to know."

Sue-Ann snored and resettled against Durwood's boot.

He said, "Talk to Jay Hogan."

The mayor clasped her hands together hopefully. "That's all I'm asking. Find out where we stand."

Durwood thought about the crop fields he'd seen riding into town. The dusty homesteads. The billboards—the dentist, the man who wanted to be sheriff. He thought of the factories still putting out smoke. For now.

The stakes were lower than what he fought for alongside Quaid and Molly McGill with Third Chance Enterprises. The planet itself was not imperiled. He wasn't likely to face exotic technologies or need to jump from moving aircraft. So it went with these injustice cases—with injustice in general. Ordinary folks suffering ordinary hardship.

"We did drive a couple thousand miles," he said. "I suppose it makes sense to stay and have a word with Mr. Hogan."

Carol Bridges rushed forward and pressed his calloused hands in her smooth ones. She gave him the address of Hogan Consolidated from memory.

CHAPTER THREE

Hogan's main factory and corporate headquarters were in the same building. Durwood parked in a visitor's spot, and he and Sue walked up to the fifth floor where the executive offices were—over the factory. Stairs were murder on the dog's hip, but she persevered. Durwood stopped every few steps for her.

Through the stairwell's glass wall, he watched the assembly line. Men and women in hard hats leaned into machine handles. A foreman frowned at a clipboard. Belts and treads and rotors turned. Even behind glass, Durwood could smell grease.

Nothing amiss here.

On the fifth floor, Durwood consulted a directory to find Jay Hogan's office.

His secretary wore nicer clothes than Carol Bridges. Looking at her neat painted fingernails, Durwood doubted she kept dog biscuits in her desk.

"You—you honestly thought bringing a *dog* to see the chief executive of Hogan Consolidated was acceptable?"

the woman said, looking at Sue's spots like they were open sores. "OSHA would have a field day if they showed up now."

Sue-Ann laid her chin on her paws.

Durwood said, "She can stay here while I see Mr. Hogan."

The woman's nameplate read *Priscilla Baird*. Durwood suspected she'd be taller than him if she stood. Her lips were tight, trembling like she was about to eject Durwood and Sue—or flee herself.

"I don't know that you will see Mr. Hogan today," she said. "You're not on his schedule. *Jones*, did you say?"

She checked her screen.

"Won't find me in your computer," Durwood said. "Is he here?"

Priscilla Baird glanced at her boss's door, which was closed.

"He is...on-site. But I'm not at liberty to say when he'd be available to speak with arbitrary members of the public."

"I'm not arbitrary. I'm here on authority of the mayor."

"The mayor?"

"Of Chickasaw, yes, ma'am. Carol Bridges."

Priscilla Baird rolled her eyes at this. Durwood thought he heard, "Getting desperate," under the woman's breath.

Durwood waited. After thirty minutes, he tired of Priscilla Baird's dirty looks and took Sue-Ann out to the van. She didn't like dogs, fine. He wouldn't be difficult just for the sake of it.

He returned to wait more. The lobby had an exposed beam running down its center—pimpled, showy. Folks built like that nowadays. Slate walls displayed oil paintings of the company's executives. Sitting out on tables were *Us*

Weekly and *Field & Stream*. Durwood read neither. He spent the time thinking of questions to ask Jay Hogan.

All told, he waited an hour and a half. Others entered and were admitted to see Hogan. Men wearing pinstripes. A made-up woman in her late forties with a couple minions hustling after her. Some kid in a ballcap and shorts carrying two plastic bags.

The kid left Hogan's office without his bags.

Durwood caught him at the door. "Pardon, youngster. What did you drop off?"

The kid ducked so Durwood could read his hat.

Crepes-a-Go-Go.

An involuntary growl escaped Durwood's mouth. He crossed to Jay Hogan's door.

"Excuse me," Priscilla Baird said. "Mr. Hogan's schedule today is terribly tight, you'll need to be patient if—"

"It just opened up," Durwood said.

He jerked the knob and blew inside. Jay Hogan was stuffing a crepe into his face with a plastic fork. Ham and some cheese that stank. The corner of his mouth had a red smear, either ketchup or raspberry jam.

Probably jam.

"The hell is this?" Hogan said. "You—what...Priscilla..." He placed a hand over his scrawny chest and finished swallowing. "Who is this person?"

Priscilla Baird rushed to the door. "I never admitted him, he went himself. He forced his way in!"

Durwood stood in the center of the office. He said to Hogan, "Let's talk, the two of us."

The young CEO considered the proposal. He was holding his crepe one-handed and didn't seem to know where to set it down. He looked at his secretary. He looked at Durwood. His hair was slicked back with Pennzoil, his skin alabaster white—a shade you'd have to stay inside to keep in southwest Texas.

Durwood extended his hand. "I can hold your pancake."

Jay Hogan stiffened at the remark. "Who are you?"

"Name's Durwood Oak Jones."

Hogan tried saying it himself. "Du*uur*wood, is it?"

"Correct." Durwood assumed Jay Hogan, like the mayor, wasn't a *Soldier of Fortune* subscriber. "I'm a concerned party."

"What does that mean?" Hogan said. "Concerned about what?"

"About this town. About the financial standing of your company."

As Priscilla Baird excused herself, Durwood explained his contact to date with Carol Bridges and the capacity in which he'd come: to investigate and combat injustice. There was no reason he and Jay Hogan shouldn't be on the same side. If the lawyers were fleecing Hogan Consolidated or Wall Street sharks were sabotaging it, Durwood's help should be appreciated.

But Jay Hogan wasn't rolling out the welcome wagon.

"*Injustice?*" he sneered. "The company's in a crap situation, a real hole. Not my fault. I didn't build those hinges. I didn't, you know, invent P/E ratios or whatever other metrics we aren't hitting."

Durwood glared across the desk. Every "not" and "didn't" stuck in his craw.

He said, "What do you do, then?"

"I chart the course," Hogan said. "I set the top-line strategy."

"Top-line?"

"Yes. Top-line."

Durwood resettled his hat on his head. "Thought the bottom line was the important one."

Jay Hogan made a sound between flatulence and a pig's snort. "Look—we've held firm on wages, kept the unions out. Done everything in our power to stay competitive."

Durwood asked what his strategy was on those lawsuits.

"Chester handles legal matters," Hogan said.

"Who's that?"

"Chester is the COO."

Durwood raised a finger, counting out letters. "Now what's the difference between CEO and COO?"

Jay Hogan made impatient motions with his hands. "The COO is the *operating* officer. He's more involved in day-to-day business."

"Who deals with Wall Street? The moneymen?"

"Chester."

"Who handles communication? Getting word out to the citizens of Chickasaw about what's going on?"

Hogan picked up his crepe again. "Chester."

He said the name—which was prissy to begin with—in a nasal, superior tone.

Durwood's fist balled at his side. "Fella must be sharp, you trust him with all that."

"Chester's extremely smart," Hogan said. "I've known him forever—our families go back generations. We attended all the same boarding schools."

"Boyhood chums?"

Hogan frowned at the question. "Something like that."

"He's about your age, then?"

Hogan nodded.

"Couple twenty-eight-year-olds running a company that dictates the fate of a whole town." Durwood folded his arms. "Sound fair to you?"

The CEO's pale cheeks colored. "They're lucky to have us. Two Ivy League graduates blessed with business instincts. Chester Lyles was president of our fraternity, graduated magna cum laude. We could be founding star-tups in Seattle or San Francisco where you don't have to drive a hundred miles for decent food."

That name rang a bell somewhere for Durwood.

Lyles.

Recalling what Carol Bridges had said about the gully, he said, "You graduate magna cum laude?"

"I don't need to defend my qualifications to you or anyone."

Durwood nodded. "Must've just missed."

Jay Hogan stood up in a snit. He looked at his crepe again in its tissue-paper sleeve and couldn't resist. He took a quick bite and thrust a finger at the door, mouth full.

"I'm done answering your questions," he said. "As CEO, I'm accountable to a shareholder-elected board of directors, which includes presidents of other corporations, a former Treasury secretary of the United States, and several other prominent executives. They're satisfied with my performance."

"How many of them live in Chickasaw?"

Hogan barked a laugh. "They understand the financial headwinds I'm up against."

"How about those bad hinges? From what I hear, Hogan used to make quality parts."

"Another Chester question. I don't deal with quality control."

That's for sure.

Durwood saw he would get nowhere with Jay Hogan. This Chester was who he needed to find. Asking this one how the town of Chickasaw was going to shake out was like inspecting your John Deere's hood ornament to judge if you needed a new tractor.

Hogan was still pointing at the door. Finally, Durwood obliged him.

On the way out, he said, "You got families counting on this company. Families with children, mortgages, sick grandmas. They're counting on you. Hogans before you did their part. Now be a man, do yours. Rise to your duty."

Hogan didn't answer. He had more crepe in his mouth.

Walking down to the parking lot, Durwood passed the factory again. It was dark—the shift had ended while he'd been waiting for Hogan. His boots clacked around the stairwell in solitude.

He considered what ailed Hogan Consolidated and whether he could fix it. He wasn't optimistic. Oh, he could poke around and get the scoop on Chester Lyles. He could do his best working around the lies and evasions he'd surely encounter. Maybe he would find Chester's or Jay Hogan's hand in the cookie jar.

The likeliest culprit, though, was plain old incompetence. Jay Hogan belonged in an insurance office someplace —preferably far from the scissors. Instead, he sat in a corner office of a multimillion-dollar company.

Did that rise to the level of injustice? Maybe. Maybe, with so many lives and livelihoods at stake.

Durwood didn't like cases he had to talk himself into.

He was just imagining how he'd break the news to Carol Bridges if nothing much came of Chester when four men burst from the shadows and tackled him.

CHAPTER FOUR

Durwood felt himself caught in a wave of rolling thunder, blows and curses raining down upon him. A stairwell rail dug into his ribs. One of the men forced him shoulder-first to the floor, hard into the cold concrete. He took punches to the chest and face. He rolled away from the blows and got hit in the back.

A rum-barrel voice ordered, "Take him inside. Nobody'll hear in the factory."

The voice belonged to the man who'd forced Durwood down. Now the other three gripped him roughly by the shirt and blue jeans. They were big men, still in work bibs. They dragged him through a door with rubber seals. Durwood's hat fell.

Nobody turned on the lights. Durwood could only sense the towering space overhead. The smell of grease was thick, like he was drowning in a giant truck axle. The men's voices echoed erratically. Idle machines loomed like hibernating bears.

Durwood let himself be prodded along. The blows

angered him, but he didn't retaliate. Not yet. In the marines, he had learned to fight on his own terms. You fight when you're ready—under the circumstances you want.

Rum Barrel said, "Piece'a garbage," and jerked Durwood by the wrist. "Nothing but a gutless leech."

Durwood wondered what he meant by "leech" but saw no point responding. Instead, he culled his senses for a mental picture of the factory. Exits. Surfaces. Materials. Dimly, he spotted a broom leaning against a sink-soap station. The space to his right sounded larger than to his left.

The men dumped him in an open area and resumed their beating.

Durwood glimpsed the leader's shirt. A sewn-in tag read: *FOREMAN*. His hair looked like black porcupine quills, and he had no neck.

This foreman said, "Take some of this back to your big-city bosses. *Chump*."

He rammed his knuckles into Durwood's face. Pain bloomed from Durwood's nose outward. He tasted blood.

The foreman loaded up a second punch, but Durwood caught it barehanded. He pushed the fist back at the man like bad cantaloupe at a roadside stand.

"I came to help you," he said. "Help y'all. Help this town."

One man squinted and seemed confused. Before Durwood could make anything of the reaction, a hand side-swiped his knee.

He slammed to the concrete again, and absorbed more blows. He felt the toll of muscles forged in labor. Working with Quaid and Molly as part of Third Chance Enterprises, Durwood had battled henchmen, thugs, and mercenaries from six of the seven continents. Many trained at gyms—or whatever gyms were called in their native tongues. They executed precise, clinical strikes. A chop to a pressure point hurt, but it didn't have the crude, soulful intent of these attacks.

Durwood disliked beating men such as these.

They were standing over him now, muttering something about liars and phonies. They joked about his hat.

He waited for their distraction to peak. Then, drawing in breath, he struck.

"Arrrgh!" the nearest said as Durwood swept his feet.

The man dropped. Durwood used his body and the momentary confusion as cover, coiling. Then he launched at the second man.

The point of his shoulder connected first. He was a boulder rolling downhill, knocking into a tree. Durwood felt the impact through his underarm, clear into his gut. The man flew four feet backward.

Durwood emerged in a crouch. He sensed the third man coming and, planting his lead foot stiff, snapped his rear around in a kick.

His bootheel connected with the man's jaw. The hostile spun like a child's top and dropped too.

Durwood faced the foreman.

The foreman circled with flexed knees. Scowling. Panting. Looking around to see if the others were getting up.

They weren't.

"Came to the wrong town, cowboy," he said. "Maybe you rode in on a horse. We'll send y'home in a bag."

Durwood mirrored the foreman's moves, right when he stepped right, left when he stepped left. Short, chopping strides. Their personal arena was bound by an assembly-line tread and what could've been a ten-ton stamper.

Durwood did a straight feint—bold, fast. The foreman swayed to his heels and shielded his face, leaving his middle open.

Durwood drove one foot into his side. The man crumpled that way. Then Durwood, watching his opponent's defenses shift as though in stop-motion, jabbed up at the face.

The foreman staggered. His eyes glassed over and Durwood advanced, but too quickly—the man brought his knee up hard and caught Durwood's chin.

As they both reeled, the foreman taunted, "Gonna kick like a sissy? We fight with fists in Texas."

If his swollen face had allowed, Durwood would've smiled at the idea honor had anything to do with fighting. Putting another human being on the ground.

Instead of smiling, he lowered his hands.

"C'mon, then," he said. "Show me them fists."

The foreman didn't trust the target in front of him. He looked to the side. He cocked his fist but did nothing with it.

Durwood focused all his rage on a point in between the foreman's eyes. He felt his own face stretch taut. Several scrapes were bleeding. Now they bled more. He took a deliberate step forward.

Twenty inches separated them.

The foreman's mouth shrank to an angry knot. He swung.

Durwood easily ducked the haymaker. The man's momentum pitched him around in a circle, legs twisted into a pretzel.

The man floundered on his knees, spent, vulnerable. Durwood could've cold-cocked him but instead used a single finger to push him over.

The other three were in different states of recovery. They groaned and elevated their limbs. One had retched. Another whimpered he couldn't feel his toes.

Durwood said, "Who ordered this?"

The men didn't answer, but their eyes ticked toward the foreman.

Durwood placed his boot on the gasping man's chest.

He repeated, "Who ordered this?"

The foreman's missing neck seemed to hamper his breath. He tried sitting up. Durwood's boot kept him pinned.

A third time, "*Who ordered this?*"

The foreman's eyes were livid. He glared at Durwood, at Durwood's boot, at his men for not coming to his aid.

Finally, all glared out, he talked. "We aren't giving up this town to you. Damn outsiders."

Durwood said, "I was asked here by the mayor."

The foreman's hateful face didn't change, but the others looked surprised.

One asked, "Mayor Bridges?"

Durwood said yes, Carol Bridges had sent him a letter.

Another asked, "What for?"

The third man said, "Wish she'd send *me* a letter."

Once the association was established, the men turned warily to their foreman. Durwood took his boot off the man's chest.

The foreman sat up, red-faced. "I was told you worked for the plaintiffs' lawyers. Some kinda professional negotiator, trying to squeeze every last penny out of us."

"Do I look like a professional negotiator to you?" Durwood wiped a spot of blood on his blue jeans. "Who fed you that bull?"

As the others nodded along with Durwood's point, the foreman considered his response. The dark factory seemed to be waiting for it, brooding. The assembly-line tread. The stamper. The hard hats hanging on nails.

The foreman grimaced. He didn't want to tell.

When Durwood's boot raised again, though, he admitted, "Chester Lyles."

CHAPTER FIVE

The workers said they didn't know where Lyles's office was. The foreman refused to tell, even with the encouragement of Durwood's boot. This angered Durwood. He considered adding his fists to the encouragement effort. All wounds could be blamed on the scuffle.

Be fair, Durwood told himself.

Anyhow, he had a feeling he'd fight this man again in time.

He returned to the executive floor to check the directory, but saw no entry for *Chester Lyles* or *Chet Lyles* or *C. von Bigdeal Lyles the Third*.

He found Carol Bridges's card in his blue jeans pocket and called her.

"Mayor Bridges speaking," she answered. "How can I help?"

"Chester Lyles," Durwood said. "Few of his boys jumped me here at the factory. I need a word with him."

Carol Bridges suggested they touch base at her office

before he do anything. She was still working, though it was seven o'clock.

Durwood agreed.

In the Vanagon, Sue-Ann nosed around his cuts and scrapes. He used the visor mirror to check his face. Left eye swollen, gash at the corner of his mouth. Not too bad. He was surely black and blue underneath his shirt and jeans, but Durwood didn't figure on Carol Bridges seeing there.

At city hall, he let Sue-Ann find a patch of lawn to make water. Then he entered. The building was empty except for a single guard.

Durwood passed through dark hallways to the mayor's office. She sat at her desk reading from a binder, head propped by the elbow.

"Nose to the grindstone," he observed.

Carol Bridges looked up. She didn't flinch at Durwood's wounds.

"Retraining programs," she said, running her finger up the binder's contents. "If these Hogan jobs go, our people still need to feed their families. I have to get them into different lines of work."

Durwood walked closer. He couldn't read the glossy pages upside down but glimpsed a picture of an eighteen-wheel rig. "Trucking?"

She nodded. "Those are the companies hiring right now. The retraining isn't bad. Six months and you're ready."

Her lips, though, were turned down.

Durwood said, "Must be a catch."

"There always is. You can retrain everyone to drive, fine, but how long do those jobs last? In five years, half these trucks could be...you know...oh, how do you say it? With the computers?"

"Autonomous," Durwood said.

Carol Bridges chuckled. "I was going to say driverless. You got the fancier word on me."

"That's me," Durwood said. "Mr. Fancy."

She reclined in her seat and took in the sight of him. Starting at the bent brim of his hat, down over the swollen eye and bloodied shirt, to the blue jeans that felt stiff as sheet metal.

Durwood took the mayor in too. Still handsome, but tired now. Hair tumbled into her cheeks. Eyelids closing over big brown eyes, then opening, putting Durwood in mind of the pretty mares he'd tended as a boy at the Jessup farm.

She talked first. "So, Chester Lyles. The people who did this"—she gestured to his eye—"worked for him?"

Durwood said, "They claimed to."

Her lip twisted darkly. "I'd hoped the Lyleses might be our allies."

Durwood thought about that notion he'd had in Jay Hogan's office that the name was familiar. "Who are they, the Lyles?"

"It's the other big family in town, besides Hogan," Carol Bridges said. "They made their fortune in oil, though it's said the wells around here ran dry in the nineties. Guess they put plenty away."

"Lyles Community Outreach Center," Durwood recalled from the drive in.

"That's them," she said. "There's a Lyles children's theater, and a shelter for battered women. The mother owns Peaceful Beans."

"The cafe? Chester Lyles's mother owns that?"

The mayor nodded.

"Hm," he said. "Big progressives."

She smiled, seeming amused by Durwood's choice of words. "The Lyleses love their causes, that's for sure. But they walk the walk. They've stuck around Chickasaw instead of moving on to greener pastures like the Hogans."

Durwood tried fitting this new information in his head.

"Why's one of their people wanting to rough me up?" he said. "Nothing peaceful about what happened back at the factory."

He gave a full account of the fight, being ambushed, the foreman with the rum-barrel voice. The men's reluctance to tell him where Chester Lyles's office was.

Carol Bridges held his gaze through most of the tale, but now her shoulders twitched. She looked past Durwood for just for a moment.

He said, "Is something happening on my six?"

She smiled at the military reference. "No, just Deputy Gomez." She crooked her finger out to the hall and called, "Alonso, come in. I know you've been wanting to."

A man shuffled out from behind the doorjamb wearing a pale-brown uniform, *Chickasaw Police Department*. He walked stooped over like there was a bunny nearby he was afraid of spooking.

He gaped at Durwood. "Mr. Oak Jones, wow! The mayor said you came, but I guess I...I didn't believe it till now. Till I saw you in the flesh. It's really you."

Sue-Ann had been sleeping. The man's busy shoes woke her now. She looked at Durwood and yawned.

"It's me," Durwood confirmed.

The men faced each other. The deputy was having trouble breathing, looked like a guppy out of its tank.

Durwood encountered fans from time to time, enthusiasts who'd seen his press clippings. The *Military Heritage* profile. The feature in *Defense News* on his legendary sniper shot, which had taken out a Rivard LLC drone seconds before it hit the fuselage of a jumbo jet carrying six heads of state.

Quaid Rafferty was always nudging some media bigwig to run a story about Third Chance Enterprises—over Durwood's objections.

"We're freelance operatives," Durwood would say. "We aren't kids hustling the neighborhood for lawns to mow, houses to paint."

Quaid would answer that marketing was the universal yoke of entrepreneurship—whether craftsman, middleman, or solicitor, in high times and in low, forever and anon.

Then Durwood would lose interest.

The mayor said, "Mr. Jones was just explaining he had a run-in down at the factory. He was attacked by men working for Chester Lyles."

Deputy Gomez took a second look at Durwood, lingering on the ex-marine's wounds.

"Bet they got the worst of it, didn't they?" he said. "Bet you whipped 'em good."

Durwood left the question unanswered. He asked Carol Bridges, "Where can I find Lyles?"

The mayor's bosom rose in a breath, and her tone was cautioning. "I do know where his office is. But before I give you that information, we need to establish some rules of engagement."

Durwood said, "His men engaged me. Few places."

"No. *No.*" Carol Bridges's eyes hardened—and now looked less like a pretty mare's than a fiery stallion's. "You will not storm the chief operating officer of Hogan Consolidated like Rambo, hell-bent on revenge. Not in my service."

Sue-Ann scooted closer to Durwood.

He smiled innocently. "I'll ask some questions. Some polite questions."

The mayor stood and pinned her hands to her hips. Off to the side, Deputy Gomez breathed in short huffs.

Finally, Carol Bridges said, "Lyles works downtown. In the new industrial park."

Durwood said he'd driven through downtown earlier on his way into town and didn't recall a park.

"*Industrial* park," she repeated. "It isn't much, honestly. We're trying to revitalize the central business district. Create some mixed-use space, offer tax breaks."

Durwood said, "Saw the one hotel."

"The Sawyer House, yes. The industrial park is right next door. Chester and Jay Hogan made a stink about Chickasaw not having a 'top-tier hotel' to accommodate out-of-town visitors. So we built the Sawyer."

"Looked nice."

"Oh, it's spectacular. There's a garden atrium, two inner courtyards. State-of-the-art fitness facility. Four-star steakhouse. Solar panels on the roof."

"Solar?" Durwood said.

Carol Bridges seemed to take this as a criticism. "We're trying. The tax base had been eroding for fifteen years running when I took office. We're playing catch-up."

Her face flushed as she spoke.

Durwood had meant nothing by the comment. Born and raised in coal country, he didn't think much of alternative energy. Wind, solar. Everyone starts riding a bike to the store, all of a sudden no more global warming.

"I've seen dying towns," Durwood said. "Folks give up, place goes to seed." He pushed his hat up his head. "There's a will here. That will starts with you."

Carol Bridges brushed a strand of hair off her cheek. "Thank you."

Durwood felt a soft twist in his middle. "I head over to this park now, will Chester be hard to find?"

"I wouldn't imagine," she said. "Like I said, Hogan's offices are just next door to the Sawyer House. You could ask the front—"

"The lawyers!" Deputy Gomez stepped between them quick as a cricket. "The lawyers're all staying at the hotel— you could see them too. Interrogate them."

The word made Durwood's skin crawl. *Lawyers.*

He said, "Now what's the lawyers' angle?"

Carol Bridges started to answer, but the deputy beat her to it. "Money, what else? They're cheating us *blind*—they are, Mr. Durwood! Er, Mr. Jones. Mr. Oak Jones. I heard they're charging Hogan double, sometimes *triple*, their usual hourly rate."

"Triple?"

The deputy nodded eagerly. "A thousand dollars an hour, I heard. This top lady, I guess the big-shot partner? She's fifteen hundred."

Durwood let those figures knock around his head. You read the news, you get used to the excess. But *fifteen hundred an hour*. To push paper and dream up excuses.

He asked, "Why would Hogan allow such a thing?"

"They're in on it! It's all a racket, Chester Lyles wants a job with them after Hogan goes bankrupt, all he's doing is—"

"Deputy Gomez," the mayor interrupted. "Let's allow

Mr. Jones to gather his own facts. He doesn't need to hear every rumor that's been around the office watercooler. Perhaps you'll give us a moment alone?"

The deputy bobbed his head and left. On his way out, though, he bugged his eyes suggestively at Durwood.

Durwood hitched his thumbs into his belt loops. "I guess we'll git, then." He showed Sue-Ann two knuckles, and she picked herself up off the floor.

Carol Bridges rushed around her desk. "Wait! We didn't have our talk about rules of engagement. If you go at Chester Lyles guns blazing, he'll just clam up."

"I've opened a clam or two."

She gripped his biceps. "I know your history—Deputy Gomez explained. About Tikrit. How you obliterated that terror cell against your CO's orders."

Durwood looked down, wrists crossed over his belt.

"Chickasaw, Texas, is a tough place," Carol Bridges continued. "We know eggs get broken when you cook an omelet. But there is a limit, Mr. Jones."

Durwood said, "Understood."

She didn't release his arm. "I brought you here. I wrote that letter. Which means your actions reflect directly on me."

Emotion rippled through her words. Durwood heard strength in them, and gravity, and the start of trust.

Maybe.

"I respect that," he said. "I do. I won't forget."

He reached across his body to pry Carol Bridges's fingers off his sleeve. They didn't want to come up, like sticky heat in the Appalachian summer.

CHAPTER SIX

Passing through downtown opposite how he'd come before, Durwood did notice signs for the industrial park. *ChixIndiePrk* written in artsy lopsided letters. Underneath, a stick-figure man held a stick-figure briefcase. Unless that was supposed to be his lunch.

Durwood parked in front of the Sawyer House. His boot's sole had barely touched asphalt when Sue whimpered.

Her mottled nose edged over the center console.

"We've been put on notice, no Rambo stuff," Durwood said. "Can you be civil?"

The dog's eyes brightened like "civil" was some new flavor of rawhide chew.

He supported her forequarters down out of the van, and they headed for the industrial park. The park abutted the hotel's south face and continued on, a few healthy bait casts farther.

Durwood couldn't figure where you got "park" from.

Two warehouses and a squat building with the Hogan logo —a rock with the letter *H* chipped into it.

There was no swing set around, no reflecting pool. Heck, if there was grass between the three buildings, he didn't see it.

Sue-Ann, who hadn't worn a leash since her puppy days, got distracted and fell back a step. Durwood sucked in sharply. Old age was no excuse for disobedience.

Then he smelled the meat himself.

Boone's Chophouse occupied the hotel's first floor. Durwood could see inside, around creamy curtains tied back with gold doodads. There was a chandelier of glittering rectangles—could've been a hundred. Servers walked with perfectly straight backs, rushing silver domes to tables. The folks doing the eating had easy smiles all around.

"Well," Durwood said, considering his dog. "I suppose every animal has their limit."

The smell was heavenly. It wasn't one smell. The buttery cow meat, sure, but pepper and potato too. And those greasy bits off the grill grate—caramel color, soft and hard at the same time.

Durwood was just preparing to snap his fingers—a command Sue wouldn't ignore in a hurricane—when he saw Chester Lyles.

Chester Lyles's smile was the easiest in the joint.

Durwood recognized the man from the executive portraits outside Jay Hogan's office. Tanned. Wavy blond hair. He resembled Quaid Rafferty in a way, but younger. And the eyes showed none of his partner's generosity and belief.

A server laid a cloth over his wrist, showed Lyles the label of a wine bottle.

Lyles sniffed his approval. The server filled all nine glasses around the table.

Wonder how this one fits in down at the outreach center, Durwood thought.

He recognized the woman at Chester Lyles's left too. The only woman of the nine. She'd been at Jay Hogan's office earlier, with minions. The minions were here too. They didn't take a sip of their wine, waiting on their boss to sip first.

She was elegant, this Boss Lady. Her suit fit like fur on a bison. Durwood doubted you could find a garment of such quality within a hundred miles of Elk Garden, if at all in the state of West Virginia.

He looked up the road, up Main Street. The rest of downtown was hurting. Windows covered in plywood. A streetlight dangling by its wires. An auto-parts store missing half its sign.

While Chester Lyles and his party ate their fillets and sized up a coffin for the town of Chickasaw.

He backtracked to the restaurant entrance. Sue followed. When the revolving door stuck, Durwood felt like driving his boot through the glass.

He stopped himself.

A hostess moved her slim fingers along the sides of a podium.

"How may I assist you, sir?"

Durwood said, "There's a man inside I need to speak with."

"Certainly. If you'd be kind enough to provide a description, I can—"

"I see him."

Durwood breezed by the podium. Seeing a dog, the hostess got a look on her face like the toilet was running over.

"We'll be brief," Durwood said.

His strides were straight and brisk. Sue-Ann trotted to keep pace. The restaurant was huge, with a ten-story ceiling and hotel rooms overlooking all four sides.

Other diners looked, edging back from their plates. The clatter of silverware faded.

When Chester Lyles saw Durwood, he paused a bite of something gray and squishy. Could've been an oyster.

He narrowed his eyes. Then he ate the bite.

Boss Lady was talking, facing away from Durwood. As he and Sue approached, she kept talking. Loud, making crisp gestures. She wore her hair in a perfect coif, brown with the very first streaks of gray.

The minions watched Durwood coming. They held their wineglasses at their lips, like police behind riot shields.

Durwood caught what he could of Boss Lady's words. It wasn't easy. She talked fast and interrupted herself. She was explaining about clauses and guarantees, and touched Chester Lyles's sleeve when she said "contingency claim."

Of all this, Durwood understood little. But he did know what sort of people used language like this, a hundred dollars of words for every nickel of truth.

Lawyers.

CHAPTER SEVEN

Boss Lady finally noticed her audience wasn't listening. She turned to see what had distracted them, and her green eyes locked on to Durwood's grays. Words kept spilling out of her mouth, finishing whatever point she'd been making like a mower sputtering down after you killed the gas.

Chester Lyles said, "Excuse me, Sybil. I believe this gentleman wants a word with us."

"Not words," Durwood said. "I'm here for answers."

He scanned the table. Besides Lyles and the lawyers—Sybil and her minions—there was a third group led by an older man who sat back fingering his cuff links. This man was round in the middle with a neat snow-white mustache. He didn't wear a monocle, but his face would've taken one perfectly.

Sue-Ann had found her way underneath the table, after a bread scrap.

Chester Lyles regained his easy grin. "You must be that man Mayor Bridges brought in." To the others: "It seems our good mayor has taken the liberty of hiring her own consultant." His eyes chuckled. "Of sorts."

The others chuckled with their mouths.

The COO formally introduced himself and asked Durwood's name. "My assistant told me, but I believe I misheard."

"Durwood Oak Jones."

Lyles centered a silk tie over his dress shirt buttons. "Apparently, I heard right. Now. How is it we can help you do your work?"

The man had a warm, accommodating manner—like he was eager to hear your thoughts. Different from Jay Hogan, who'd acted hostile and superior.

Durwood preferred the latter. He'd take a loudmouth rooster over a snake in the grass every time.

"I'm here to find out what's to become of Hogan," he said. "Folks in this town depend on Hogan. They've put their sweat and tears into it. They deserve to know."

Sybil, the lawyer boss, got real interested in the tines of her fork. Mustache Man made sure his napkin covered his stomach.

Chester Lyles said, "I can assure you, everyone sitting around this table understands the gravity of the situation. Hogan Consolidated has a long, proud history, clear back to the 1920s, of paying an honest wage for an honest day's work. Our guiding principle is to do right by that legacy. To find a resolution to the current crisis that honors the sanctity of labor."

Something about these words, slipping one after another from his mouth, made Durwood think of missiles on a mute night-vision feed tumbling out the belly of a bomber.

Durwood said, "What is the resolution?"

The direct question tripped Lyles. "That's, uh—it's still taking shape. We're working tirelessly to balance shareholder value with the best interests of Chickasaw."

The others watched Durwood, wondering whether he'd be appeased.

Durwood gestured to Mustache Man. "Who's he?"

The man chuckled at not being recognized. "Rudyard Raines, Raines Financial Services."

He tottered up and extended his hand. They shook. Durwood's hand felt like sandpaper against the moneyman's.

More introductions were made. Young, clean folks—all worked for Raines or Sybil Fitzgerald. Most were slight and shied from Durwood's grip, but the one next to Rudyard Raines tried squeezing Durwood's hand into pulp.

"*Britt Holcomb*," he said, full of puffy gym muscles. "I think you've wandered where you don't belong, bro."

Durwood squeezed right back. The man's pink face came close to purple.

Raines put in, "No, Britt, it's fine. The restaurant is a public place. Mr. Jones is quite within his rights."

Reluctantly, Britt Holcomb pulled his hand away.

Durwood turned to Lyles. "Seems like everyone here's on the 'shareholder value' end of the teeter-totter. Who represents the town?"

Chester Lyles grinned and thumped his own chest. "Me, of course. I'm Chickasaw born and bred. My family's served this community for the better part of a century. Used to eat an ice-cream sundae every Saturday night at the Dairy Whip."

"You and Jay Hogan."

"Sure. Jay and I go back to nursery school."

"Before your folks shipped you off to boarding school."

Lyles shook his head. "*I* chose boarding school—my older brother attended Chickasaw High. I wanted more."

Durwood glanced around at the lawyers and bankers, then at the man's plate. The bare T-bone of an eaten steak sat in a dollop of creamed spinach.

"I'd say you got it."

Lyles shrugged. "It's a good thing I left and got the best education available—it put me on equal footing with these killers." He winked around the group. "Helps me negotiate the best possible terms for Chickasaw."

Durwood said, "And what terms are those?"

Lyles looked at Rudyard Raines. The older man gave back a look Durwood couldn't read.

"By rights, I shouldn't be discussing this," Lyles said. "These are sensitive financial detai—"

"You shouldn't'a sicced your goons on me."

The table held its breath at the interruption. The only sound was Sue-Ann's tongue on the hardwood below.

Lyles recovered. "Clearly, Durwood, you're in a special category—and we want to keep you and the mayor in the loop. It'll be a matter of public record soon, anyway." He shook out his sleeves. "Hogan Consolidated is selling itself to Raines Financial. Rudyard here has generously agreed to purchase the company for forty-six cents on the dollar, which allows us—"

"Forty-four," Raines corrected.

Lyles made a jokey headlock motion. "We're still hammering out the details. Wherever we end up, they'll be assuming all legal jeopardy pertaining to pending litigation against Hogan."

Durwood said, "Those bum hinges?"

"The hinges, yes," Lyles said. "Our PVC flanges have had issues as well."

As the discussion moved to industrial parts, the lawyer minions and Raines's underlings got bored. They took out their phones or ate more of their food.

Except Britt Holcomb, who kept eyeing Durwood like he wanted to meet out back.

Well? Durwood supposed he had his answer. The company was being sold because it couldn't afford to pay out the lawsuits. Carol Bridges had more or less guessed it. How Raines Financial would proceed was unclear. Would they close the factories and sell off assets, fire everyone? Or take an honest shot at running the business?

Looking into Rudyard Raines's eyes, set deep in his face like buttons in a couch, Durwood wasn't betting on honest anything.

He said, "Hogan built quality parts for a century, now they can't drive a straight nail. That it?"

Chester Lyles sighed. "Things change, what can I tell you? The workforce gets soft, lazy. It just happens."

Durwood said, "Nothing just happens."

The others tittered. They thought he was simple. They saw the dog, saw the hat, figured they had Durwood Oak Jones pegged.

Rudyard Raines said, "We have tremendous respect for the employees of Hogan Consolidated. We plan to take a hard look at things before making any determination of next steps. We'll be crunching all the numbers."

Sue-Ann, done fishing for scraps, returned to Durwood's side. He smoothed her floppy ear.

"You've already done your crunching," he said. "That's how you got to forty-four."

Nobody disputed this. Sybil Fitzgerald hid a smirk behind her napkin.

Durwood nodded out the window. "Chickasaw deserves more than lip service."

Chester Lyles peeked at a silver wristwatch. "I don't know what more to say, friend. We've run up against financial reality. Facts are facts."

"They oughta be," Durwood agreed. "But folks at the top have a way of picking and choosing which facts matter."

Sybil Fitzgerald leaned forward into the fray. "Have you considered the source of *your* facts, Mr. Jones? Have you considered that Mayor Bridges might have ulterior motives of her own?"

Durwood felt weight shift to his bootheels.

Lyles seized the point. "Sybil's right, one thousand percent. Bridges got elected on a rabidly anti-corporate platform. I assume you knew that, yes?"

"We didn't talk politics."

"You didn't know she's a big Democrat? Real rising star. Thinks Hogan doesn't pay enough taxes—that was a big part of her campaign."

Durwood had assumed the mayor to be Republican, this part of the state.

He said, "She struck me as a fair woman."

But even saying this, Durwood felt doubt. Maybe Carol Bridges was using him. Maybe that humble smile and those legs, crossing and uncrossing, had been part of a ruse—a scheme to get her reelected or up to the next rung.

More troubling was the doubt Durwood felt toward himself. He'd hated lawyers for as long as he could remember. His father had called them "the scourge of society" and gritted his teeth every time some ambulance chaser's commercial played on their twelve-inch Zenith.

Had this prejudice blinded Durwood? Made him see crimes where an impartial man wouldn't have?

The bankers and lawyers looked more relaxed, Durwood saw now. They'd read him. They knew they'd brushed him off the plate.

"You say it'll be public record soon." Durwood looked at Chester Lyles. "When's the deal go final?"

"Friday," the COO said. "Close of business, five o'clock sharp."

Durwood's hand found the top of Sue's head again. He started them for the door.

Two days.

CHAPTER EIGHT

Durwood checked into a motel on the outskirts of town. The motel had two levels, skinny balconies, and a flat roof. He parked the van where he could keep an eye on it from the room.

He hadn't eaten. Durwood often skipped or forgot meals when he was working. Now his stomach felt like it wanted to chew through his shirt, so he got chips from a vending machine. Then he fed Sue-Ann from the steel drum of chow they traveled with—stowed between the frag grenades and cased Dragunov sniper rifle.

Afterward, he lay down on the stiff bedspread to think. His body ached. One kneecap looked crooked.

Two days.

The key to the case, Durwood believed, was Chester Lyles. Jay Hogan had ceded all meaningful authority to him. Was Lyles representing Hogan Consolidated in good faith, or cooking up a deal to line his own pockets?

Durwood knew you couldn't unzip a man like some smuggler's duffel bag and judge what lay inside. Heck, he'd known Quaid Rafferty a decade and still hadn't pegged him good from bad.

What you could do, though, was look hard at where a man came from.

Durwood set a bowl of water out for Sue and drove to Peaceful Beans.

The cafe had a lively appearance. Flashing colors chased around the neon *OPEN* sign. A porcelain frog wearing a top hat, the size of a large child, welcomed patrons at the front door. Durwood parked next to a beater Plymouth with a *BYODESL* license plate and a bumper sticker that read: *This car is a vegetarian.*

Two steps into the cafe, Durwood was shouted at by an older lady behind the register.

"No weapons of any kind, sir!" she said. "Sign's right out front."

Durwood turned. Sure enough, there was a window sticker showing a red line over the outlines of a gun and knife. "I understood Texas to be an open carry state."

He moved his jacket to show that his M9 was properly holstered.

The woman, whose tall face and sharp, skinny nose gave her the look of a peeved bird, said over a customer's head, "You understand correct. But gun violence costs our great state four thousand souls and sixteen billion dollars annually, so I'll ask you respectfully to abide our rules rather than those of a legislature that's seventy-seven percent male, sixty-four percent white, and one hundred percent in the NRA's pocket."

Durwood knew folks felt strongly on the matter. He locked his gun in the van.

Back inside the cafe, he found the woman done with her

customer and smiling beside a second lady. Both could've been in their sixties.

"Thank you kindly. Now Nina and I"—she nodded to the other—"can prepare your no-foam double soy latte without fear of overfrothing and incurring your wrath."

"I only drink coffee in the morning," Durwood said.

The woman spread her arm with a flourish over a pastry case. "Then you must've popped in for one of our scrumptious gluten-free flourless brownies."

Durwood squinted at the treats, which did look fine—petite, dusted with powdered sugar. "You're the owner, I take it?"

She nodded.

He said, "I'm here to ask some questions about your son."

The woman's eyes cut to a corner table, where a man in a surplus jacket was drawing with a red marker.

"If you have questions about Joad," she said, "you can ask him yourself. Nina and I don't monitor every last thing that happens in our cafe."

"Joad?" Durwood said. Before the woman could respond, he continued, "I meant your other son. Chester Lyles."

The woman's sharp nose seemed to get sharper. She looked down.

Durwood said, "Isn't he your son?"

"He is, yes. Much to his chagrin."

Durwood looked between the women. Nina was shorter than Chester Lyles's mother and wore a beaded necklace. Both were lean with tan, weathered skin.

"Take it you, uh"—Durwood tapped the thigh of his blue jeans—"had Chester under a different configuration?"

Nina's gaze narrowed, but her partner seemed to get a kick out of his question. She regarded Durwood for a moment. She seemed to probe his steel-gray eyes.

"I spent my middle three decades playing a part," she said. "Domestic guardian of the Lyles legacy, bearer and educator of its heirs. The bubble had to pop before I could see what I truly wanted." She sighed. "I'm Evelyn Sandecker-Lyles. Call me Evie."

Durwood shook her offered hand and gave his own name. "What's this bubble that popped?"

Evie continued her probing look. "You're the guy Carol wrote a letter to? From West Virginia?"

Durwood noticed a *Carol Bridges for Mayor* sign on the wall beside a picture of her and Evie.

"Yes, ma'am."

She looked at Nina for a beat. Her partner nodded.

"Not many know," she said. "Even Carol—she's too polite to ask. The truth is the Lyles fortune ran out. My ex-husband, all his siblings—they acted like we could keep on funding the arts, sustaining at-risk communities, and the oil money would last indefinitely. It was fantasy."

Durwood nodded to the man with the marker. "How old were your boys when the money trouble hit?"

"Joad was nineteen, Chester only sixteen." She looked around the cafe, forlorn. "Is that all it's been, twelve years? Feels like twelve lifetimes."

Over a tumbler of kombucha, Evie recounted how her husband had packed up his easel and brushes and hopped a flight to Belize—leaving her to face the creditors and explain their new reality to the kids.

"We all responded in our own way," she said. "I opened Peaceful Beans to make ends meet, and found Nina." The women clasped hands atop the counter. "Horace Jr.—he goes by Joad now—stayed on the same track of social justice, but Chester..."

Durwood said, "Joined the dark side."

Evie chuckled, joyless. "He and Jay Hogan were already close. He rebelled against me, always had. He found the Hogans' worldview seductive. It was different from what he'd heard growing up."

"Were the families hostile toward each other?"

"Not at all," she said. "Both families supported Chickasaw. Still do. Nowadays, the Hogans are the ones mostly footing the bill for the museums, the soup kitchen. But they keep our names on the signs, stay out of the day-to-day management. Just like we always stayed out of their business, running Hogan Consolidated."

"Until Chester," Durwood said.

"Right," Evie said. "I think money played into that, him taking the COO job. There at the beginning, after my husband left but before I had my bearings, it was rough. We moved into a duplex. Their friends were asking questions— the cat almost got out of the bag several times. I think Chester didn't want to feel that way ever again. That vulnerable."

Durwood was no expert on vulnerability, but he could imagine going from penthouse to poorhouse would have an effect. Make a man bitter.

He looked over at Joad, the other son. It seemed he'd finished drawing. Now he was stapling fliers onto wood stakes.

Joad saw him looking and called, "You're here to stop Hogan, right? Make justice?"

Durwood ambled over to read the fliers.

Green Factories = Healthy Worker Lungs.

$7.25 Texas Minimum Wage? Noooo: WE CAN DO BETTER. Negotiations START at $14.50!

He recalled Jay Hogan's words about staying competitive, holding the line on wages.

"You're organizing some protest," he said.

"Absolutely." Joad's voice was hoarse with zeal. "Now's the time for change, when everybody's drawing up terms. Labor deserves a seat at the table."

"Maybe," Durwood said. "But maybe seeing rabble-rousing and such, if you're an investor thinking to put money into Hogan, you get scared off."

"Good." Joad spread his shoulders. "I *hope* we chase off those too timid for progress."

Durwood looked at him, the troublemaker. He had a mop of hair and his mother's tall face, which gave him the appearance of an overstuffed trash bin.

"You drive the veggie car?" Durwood said, nodding outside.

Joad neatened his stack of fliers. "Somebody in this town needs to think about emissions."

Durwood caught a whiff of alcohol on his breath and decided not to waste his own.

He said, addressing both the mother and son, "Y'all know Chester best. Is he crooked? Would he sell Chickasaw down the river?"

Joad rolled his eyes like the question was beneath him.

Evie's expression was thoughtful. Nina stood behind, a bracing hand on her shoulder blade.

"I want to say no way, he never woould." Evie winced. "But it's been years since we've... I mean, he used to be caring—quite a caring boy. I remember in orchestra he would help Trisha Peters carry her French horn. I love him. I love him, and I pray to God he remembers the values Horace and I..."

As she trailed off, Durwood felt a weakness in his jaw. He wished Molly McGill were here. His Third Chance partner was trained in psychology, skilled at reading people. She would've known what to say to Evie. She would've had insights into Chester Lyles, what it all meant. The downfall of his family. Why he'd adopted such contrary values to his mother's.

Molly could've said what sort of man Durwood was dealing with.

Several teens had entered the cafe after Durwood. They were milling behind him now, reading the chalkboard menu.

Durwood said to Evie, "I should buy something." He felt he owed the woman for her time.

Evelyn Sandecker-Lyles brushed away a tear. She gestured to the pastry case again, but without the flourish.

Durwood's stomach lurched at the choices—all he'd eaten today was the bag of chips.

"I will try one of those brownies, please," he said. "They taste okay without the gluten? No flour?"

Evie smiled, using tongs to pick up the first in a line of the bars. "Your gastrointestinal system will thank you for it."

Durwood rarely conversed with his body, which seemed to do alright on whatever he put in. He took the brownie to go and decided, next, to call his own son.

CHAPTER NINE

In the marines, Durwood had learned the importance of knowing your enemy. You couldn't plan a strike or defense without understanding what reaction you were likely to provoke—the tendencies of your adversary.

Durwood knew a fair bit of Chester Lyles's story now but virtually nothing about Rudyard Raines and Sybil Fitzgerald.

Were their interests aligned? Was bilking Hogan for fees the endgame, or did they have grander plans?

Durwood had no way to think about these questions. The weapons in play weren't IEDs or roadside ambushes but injunctions, earnings reports, stock options—tools Durwood had no grasp of.

But Luke did.

Durwood's wife and eldest son had served, as Durwood had, in the military. They'd died in the military—Maybelle at the terrorists' hands in Tikrit, Cade training to be a naval aviator at Miramar.

His younger son, Luther, had bucked at how he and

Maybelle raised him. Luther had refused to join ROTC in high school and gone away to the Northeast for college. After graduation, he'd taken a job with Goldman Sachs.

There was no bitterness between them, nothing like Evie and Chester. The last time Durwood had seen Luke—he went by "Luke" now—was a couple Christmases ago, after he and Quaid had defused the antimatter bomb on top of the Empire State Building. They simply had different lives. Different interests.

Back at the hotel, Durwood found Luke's number in his cell-phone log from the day after Father's Day.

"Dad, hey, out of the blue," Luke answered on the fifth ring. "Tell me you're not calling from the lair of some madmen planning to annihilate half the world's population."

"I'm in Texas," Durwood said.

His son laughed. "I can see you in Texas."

"Are you home?"

"Nah, I'm at the office—we're slammed pounding out this IPO issue for a client. It's due tomorrow. What's the scoop?"

Durwood, pacing around the motel room's desk, explained the injustice he was pursuing. He was brief, not wanting to keep Luke from his work.

"Figured you might know this Rudyard Raines fella," he said. "Or know of him."

"Rudyard Raines?" Luke repeated. "Of course, I know Rudyard Raines. Do you not? Honestly?"

Durwood said he honestly did not know the man.

His son's tone was skeptical. "This isn't you just playing your role, being all tough and disdainful about the godless modern world?"

Durwood took a moment before answering. The motel room's heat-AC unit kept spinning down its fan, then spinning back on. The thermostat was next to the door and a window—both mistakes.

"I read the *Coal Valley Times* twice a week," he said. "If they mentioned Rudyard Raines, I guess I missed it."

"How about *Forbes*, Dad? Do you ever see *Forbes* magazine, maybe lying around the public library?"

"No," Durwood said. "I don't believe ours carries it."

Luke described the magazine's April cover, titled *Doctor Cash* and featuring Rudyard Raines wearing a stethoscope of braided hundred-dollar bills.

"He just bought an airline," Luke said. "We hear he's going to reorg and spin-off the crap parts. He owns Bigga-Burger...owns Lingerie Warehouse...owns that football league that plays games in the spring."

The football league Durwood did know some about. That Mountaineers' quarterback, the short one who could really scoot, had played a few seasons.

"I thought that league went belly-up," Durwood said.

"Not quite." Luke made a sucking sound. "Raines Financial bought 'em just before the money ran out. They laid off ninety-eight percent of the employees and canceled all the games, but the legal entity still exists. They hold the real estate. They'll assert copyright or try to exploit patents the league filed previously."

Durwood waited for the terminology to quit running around his head.

"Doesn't seem like much of a business," he said.

"True," Luke said. "*Forbes* called them 'zombie subsidiaries' in the article—it's Raines's specialty. For all practical purposes, they're dead, but they continue to provide dormant revenue streams and tax shelters for the parent company."

"The parent being…"

"Raines Financial."

Durwood tried piecing this together. The only response he could manage was, "Huh."

"It's actually brilliant," Luke said. "The tax code is full of benefits to distressed corporations—Raines sort of strings them out over time, reaping the spoils with no intention of ever making the business whole."

The heat-AC fan spun down.

Durwood muttered, "Like milking a dead cow."

"Ha, I suppose so," Luke said.

"And Rudyard Raines invented this?"

"Yeah," Luke said. "Well, probably some fifth-year analyst like me dreamed it up, but yeah, Raines's firm started it. He gets the credit."

Durwood, the cell phone to his ear, tried imagining what Hogan Consolidated might look like as a zombie subsidiary. Raines would hold on to the factories for a write-off. Maybe he'd keep a skeleton staff in Chickasaw for paperwork and administrative matters.

He'd surely fire the line workers.

When Luke spoke again, his voice had more urgency. "Dad, if Raines has a deal lined up to buy this…Logan Consolidated, was it?"

"Hogan," Durwood said.

"Got it, Hogan. If Raines has a deal in the works, you aren't going to stop it. He's the best. His analysts, his lawyers—all the best. It'll be airtight."

"Maybe."

Luke gasped, sounding exasperated. "If you go after

Rudyard Raines, he's going to *eat you for lunch*. Guaranteed. This isn't a—you know, it's not some armed standoff on the polar ice caps."

"No," Durwood agreed. "It's not."

"And also, I mean just for me, I've risen pretty high up the ladder here at Goldman." Luke lowered his voice—Durwood didn't know whether he worked in an office or cubicle where there'd be people nearby. "If you make an enemy of Rudyard Raines in some big public way that reflects on me..."

He didn't finish.

Durwood said, "I don't intend to attract publicity."

"Except everything Raines does ends up on the front page of the *Wall Street Journal*."

Durwood asked if Goldman did much business with Raines Financial.

"Not really," Luke admitted, "but that's not the point. If somebody in my family appears hostile toward financial entrepreneurs, it's just not a great look."

The heat-AC unit spun on yet again in the silence. Durwood was ready to drive his bootheel through its grill.

"Financial entrepreneur," he said. "That what Rudyard Raines is? Couple pretty words there."

Luke spluttered his lips. "Fine, Dad—nobody's as pure as you. Everyone on Wall Street's evil. We're all just divvying up the old people's pensions and driving up prices on cancer drugs."

Before things could worsen, Durwood apologized for interrupting Luke's work and wished him luck with that IPO. The call ended civilly, both men pledging to catch up more soon.

Durwood walked to the bathroom and filled a glass

with tap water. He took the water to the window and stood, drinking.

The sun had set on Chickasaw, leaving behind a purplish sky. No plumes came from the smokestacks. The lone stoplight he saw was blinking red. In the distance, white specks inched along Texas-12, the highway Durwood had driven in on.

His son was right. This was Rudyard Raines's battlefield. Sybil Fitzgerald's battlefield. Not his. It wasn't the polar ice caps.

Durwood smiled. *Polar ice caps*. Luke always had been quick like that.

CHAPTER TEN

You find yourself on the wrong battlefield at times, but that doesn't mean you pack up and leave.

Durwood needed a computer. He left the motel room in search of one, hoping for a public machine in the lobby— the kind you print boarding passes and such with. No luck.

He called Carol Bridges.

"I've got a computer, sure," she said. "In my office. What'll we be using it for?"

Before answering, Durwood thought a minute. About the lawyers' and bankers' smooth words, about that *Carol Bridges for Mayor* sign at Peaceful Beans.

She hadn't lied about being a Democrat. But she hadn't been too forthright. What had she said when the topic of Peaceful Beans had come up? *The Lyleses love their causes, that's for sure.*

Durwood had taken the impression she—Carol Bridges —didn't think much of those causes. But maybe that was a poor impression. Maybe the fault lay with him.

The topic gave Durwood a headache. He disliked

parsing words. Shelving his concerns for now, he fixed the phone to his ear and told the mayor what he'd learned from Luke and at Boone's Chophouse. He explained he wanted to dig deeper into Raines Financial and Sybil Fitzgerald's law firm.

"Wait one minute," Carol Bridges said. "Raines is *buying* the company? But they've been consulting for Jay and Chester for the last three years. Isn't that a massive conflict of interest?"

Her outrage was bright through Durwood's cell phone speaker. He'd returned to the room and was gathering his jacket and keys.

"I imagine so," he said.

"And you said the lawyer was there, Sybil Fitzgerald? She knows about conflict of interest—she should've raised hell. *Why wasn't she raising hell?*"

From his years married to Maybelle, Durwood knew women sometimes asked questions they didn't want answered.

Carol Bridges continued, "This smells. Hogan has been paying these two firms exorbitant fees, letting them leech money out of our community for years. And this is their big plan—a salvage sale?"

Leaving Sue-Ann to sleep, he drove to city hall. Peaceful Beans next door was slowing down, though Joad's plant-powered Plymouth was still parked out front. The municipal lot was bare except for the mayor's truck. Deputy Gomez and the security guard must've gone home.

Carol Bridges's dark-red hair was down, hanging loose like unbraided rope about her shoulders. Seeing Durwood, she tied it up into a knot.

She made space at the keyboard. "Do you want to type or should I?"

He turned over his calloused hands. "My money's on you."

They searched for information online, first about the law firm—Fitzgerald, Combs, and Doucey—then about Raines Financial. They checked for news of Hogan Consolidated too, in case there was some nugget floating around Carol Bridges hadn't already heard.

Neither was a pro at the internet. They crinkled their brows at nonsense results. They struggled to make their way around the companies' websites, Durwood pointing hesitantly around the screen, the mayor slow with the mouse.

The first breakthrough came when they tried *Hogan Consolidated* together with *Fitzgerald, Combs, and Doucey* in a search. The top result was a five-year-old document from the United States Court of Appeals for the Fifth Circuit in New Orleans.

Carol Bridges clicked it, and they read shoulder to shoulder. It seemed several of Hogan's corporate customers had joined a price-fixing suit, claiming the company had used its market position to keep prices high. The legalese zoomed over Durwood's head, but the line at the very top —printed double the size of the rest—was clear enough.

CASE DISMISSED.

"Look it." Durwood read from the screen. "The lawyers for the defense, for Hogan, aren't Fitzgerald, Combs, and Doucey."

Carol Bridges followed his eyes to the name of a law firm based in South Texas. "They had different counsel. So why did this document show up in our search?"

Durwood didn't know.

In another minute, Carol Bridges figured how to scan the webpage for the word "Fitzgerald," and they found it clear at the bottom in a section labeled *Supplemental legal representatives for the plaintiffs*.

"For the plaintiffs?" she said. "That can't be right. Who was the primary plaintiff's attorney?"

Another Texas firm was listed as the acting attorneys for the party accusing price-fixing. Which meant Fitzgerald, Combs, and Doucey had ridden shotgun.

Durwood looked at the name of that East Coast law firm hiding at the bottom of the screen like a gator in pond grass.

He said, "Who do you figure was really calling the shots? Fitzgerald or that Podunk firm up the road?"

Carol Bridges frowned.

They found three more federal filings against Hogan. Another price-fixing case, an antitrust suit involving some decades-old purchase of an ore supplier in Wyoming, and a false advertising claim about billboards in El Paso.

All three had been dismissed. In all three, Fitzgerald, Combs, and Doucey were named as *Supplemental legal representatives for the plaintiffs*.

"They've been gunning for Hogan for years. In secret." Carol Bridges rubbed her eyes. She'd been hunched at the keyboard for a solid hour. "They couldn't make anything stick."

Durwood's own eyes felt brittle. He and the mayor twisted from the screen, both seeking relief at the same time. Their legs bumped. His shin got mixed up with her knees. Neither flinched.

They said together, "Until now."

When the moment passed, Durwood assumed the

keyboard. He searched for court documents relating to the defective hinges and flanges. There were nine, split between state and federal jurisdictions. Durwood tried scanning for "Fitzgerald" as Carol Bridges had, but came up empty.

"Dang," he said.

Carol Bridges examined the documents more closely. "They're all marked 'preliminary filings,'" she said. "Only the primary counsel is named in preliminary findings. The full records haven't been released—the cases are too recent."

Her fingers nudged Durwood's off the keys—not unpleasantly. She clicked ahead to the courts' official websites. Many were unhelpful and had no information about getting public records.

The last gave a phone number.

For details pertaining to the current docket, please telephone the court clerk.

"Telephone," Durwood said. "How quaint."

They decided she should call, a female voice less threatening and Carol Bridges a better talker besides.

Durwood watched her dial. Her tongue moved across her upper lip in concentration. Though their legs had separated, he still felt her warmth in his blue jeans.

Carol Bridges opened her mouth to speak into the receiver, then closed it.

"Straight to voice mail," she reported.

No surprise there. Government office near ten o'clock.

Durwood thought some. Then he asked, "Do Jay Hogan and Chester Lyles realize their current lawyers had it out for 'em?"

"I don't see how they couldn't," the mayor said. "Unless they're totally incompetent."

Durwood thought about sixteen-year-old Chester packing up his clothes for the duplex.

"Or in on the scam," he said.

Carol Bridges frowned again.

"Let's try calling in the morning," she said. "If we get hard confirmation that Sybil Fitzgerald's firm is playing both sides on these injury lawsuits, that's big. That changes everything."

"She knows we're on her trail," Durwood said. "Might've started covering her tracks. Better to move tonight."

"Sure, but the place is closed." She gestured good-naturedly to his face, which was a mishmash of cuts and bruises. "And look, Durwood, you need the sleep. If you don't mind me saying."

The ex-marine smiled. It was true. He hadn't gotten a wink since arriving in Chickasaw—and this after driving through the night. Durwood never had been much for sleep. Maybelle used to nag him for it.

He was about to disagree when a crash sounded from the hall.

CHAPTER ELEVEN

Durwood stood to investigate. Before he could start toward the noise, Carol Bridges held him fast by the sleeve. She tugged him to a corner out of sight from the hall.

She whispered, *"Could they have the office bugged?"*

Durwood sat poised over one knee, prepared to draw his M9. The mayor kept gripping his sleeve.

"Possibly," he said.

A company like Raines Financial or Fitzgerald, Combs, and Doucey wouldn't generally keep muscle on its payroll. When you're dealing with large sums of money, though, all bets are off. Money has a way of attracting muscle—whether you call it "Corporate Security," "Risk Mitigation," "Corporate Espionage." Whatever. It boils down to muscle.

Three quick taps sounded on the mayor's door.

Carol Bridges crawled forward to look.

"Alonso, goodness." Her bosom rose and fell in a sigh. "You scared me half to death."

She opened the door. Deputy Gomez, after apologizing

for the fright, shook Durwood's hand for the second time that day. He was still wearing his badge and uniform.

"I was just driving by and saw the van out front." His eyes shone. "The mobile Third Chance headquarters—wow! Guess I missed it before. It's a beaut."

The Vanagon sometimes made it into published reports, Durwood knew. After they'd jumped that broken span of the New River Gorge Bridge. The time it'd withstood a direct hit from Fabienne Rivard's space laser while chasing drug mules across the Mojave.

Durwood said, "She gets us where we need to go."

Carol Bridges looked between the two men with a bemused expression. She went to fix her hair knot, showing her smooth underarms.

Deputy Gomez said, "What're you guys up to, making a plan? What's the plan?"

Durwood recovered his attention. "I'm about to head back to the Sawyer House."

Carol Bridges dropped her hair.

"No, you aren't," she said. "You *can't*. You have no proof."

"That's what I'm going for," he said. "Get proof."

Deputy Gomez watched them argue like he was sitting at the fifty-yard line of a West Virginia Mountaineers football game.

The mayor said, "All they're going to do is deny, deny, deny."

Durwood tipped his head. "With their mouths. But they'll have files. Records of what they been doing."

"And you expect they're just going to hand those records over to you?"

"No." He hitched a thumb through one of his belt loops.

"Don't expect they will."

Durwood thought back to the steakhouse. Those thick embroidered napkins and buttery bites. Sybil Fitzgerald and her minions drinking that golden wine. His jaw set.

The mayor said, "What exactly are you planning to do?"

"Tell 'em we know," Durwood said. "We know they're playing both sides. They don't hand over the files, we'll expose them."

"Expose them how?"

"Well..." Durwood took in a long breath, aware he'd swum a few strokes too far from shore. "You got your fax machine. Those cities fax us the court documents in the morning, we'll send 'em ahead to the *Washington Post*."

He considered the answer clever by his own modest standard. Carol Bridges, though, wasn't impressed.

"They'll drag their feet. They'll just stall you, Durwood." She said his name with a pleading quiver. "They're going to file their motions and evade. Any mud that sticks around they'll leave to their PR people."

"PR."

"Public relations," she clarified.

Durwood was aware of the term.

She continued, "Just because we're in the right doesn't mean we'll prevail."

Durwood's mind was stuck on buttery bites and wine.

He said, *"The eyes of the Lord are on the righteous, and his ears are attentive to their cry."*

"Psalm 34:15," she said.

He felt the corners of his lips spread.

Carol Bridges ran a hand up her hip and continued, *"The prudent sees danger and hides himself, but the simple go on and suffer for it."*

"Proverbs 22:3," Durwood said. "So I'm simple, am I?"

"Not at all," she said. "Which is how I know you're going to be prudent."

They stared into each other's eyes, at an impasse.

Durwood took the mayor's point, but the fact was they had two days. The town had two days. Sometimes during difficult missions, an opening would appear—a soft unguarded belly, just for a flash. Your enemy slipped. You gained insight a tick before they did. If you failed to strike in those moments, decisively, the opening closed.

Deputy Gomez put in, "What I heard is the lawyers keep two sets of records, a box of fakes for the taxman and then another one that's legit."

Carol Bridges gave him a look.

"I have a source!" the deputy said defensively. "I do, he's inside—he says there's black boxes and plain boxes, the black ones nobody's ever allowed to see."

Durwood asked where they kept these black boxes.

"I dunno." Deputy Gomez watched his feet shuffle. "I think the hotel."

This struck Durwood as sheer conjecture. It didn't matter, though. Whatever they kept the records in, whether it was boxes or crates or a ten-ton safe, he would find it.

He announced, "I'm going."

"Durwood, *please*," Carol Bridges said.

"Can I come?" the deputy asked. "I know the Sawyer House, I know the layout—"

"No," Durwood said.

He looked into Carol Bridges's tortured face. In his life, he'd rarely found the right words in such situations. He thought now of taking her hand but didn't.

He said again, "I'm going."

CHAPTER TWELVE

The Sawyer House frontage was lit by stoneware torches with five-foot open flames. At least they looked like flames. They could've been gussied-up LEDs.

Durwood parked under a dark sky in spitting distance of a Lexus and two Mercedes-Benzes. The van looked like a hippo nosing in for a drink at the flamingo pool.

It wasn't six steps through the lobby before Durwood encountered his old pal: the foreman.

"They figured you might be back," the neckless man said. "Looking for trouble."

Durwood gestured to the foreman's swollen lip. "And they put you in charge of security? Must not be as smart as they're cracked up to be."

The foreman scratched at his buzz cut. "This hotel's private. For guests, is what that means. You a guest here?"

"I'm at the motel over town."

"Then clear off. You've got no business on the premises."

He stepped forward and raised his arm as though to

usher Durwood out. The ex-marine's face hardened. The foreman stopped short of contact.

Durwood said, "Whose dime're you on now? Are you protecting Chester Lyles, or these lawyers and bankers?"

"My paycheck comes from Hogan Consolidated. I report to Chester Lyles."

"And who's he report to?"

The foreman's jaw went tight. "Me and the boys asked about you. Mr. Lyles said you and Carol Bridges intend to interfere."

Durwood said, "What happened to me being some professional negotiator?"

They stared at each other. Durwood's gaze stayed level and unconcerned. The foreman kept picking up and setting down his feet like he was standing on a warming griddle.

"Mr. Lyles comes from good people," he said. "My little niece has Down's—the Lyleses run that center, helps my sister out."

Durwood looked at the man. He saw, instead of a puffed-up goon, an uncle pulling quarters out from behind ears.

"I can't tell you who to trust," said. "I can only tell you what I see. From the outside, it looks like Lyles and his East Coast buddies are carving up this town like a Thanksgiving bird with gravy."

He told briefly of Fitzgerald, Combs, and Doucey's involvement in the lawsuits.

"*That's lies,*" the foreman spat. "You made it up."

But Durwood caught a quiver between his eyes—there at the bridge of his nose. Durwood walked past to the elevator bank, leaving the man to his doubts.

He pushed *Up* and waited.

Between the elevators, water trickled down a glass pane into a bed of shiny black and white pebbles. Water sculpture, Durwood supposed. He couldn't tell if the water was behind or in front of the glass. Maybe that was the point. Maybe it was meant to be thought-provoking.

When a car arrived, Durwood boarded and pressed the button for Fifteen: the top floor. The elevator motor purred, quiet, smooth. As it carried him up, Durwood thought. The foreman would likely be calling in backup now, alerting Chester Lyles. That was fine. Durwood didn't expect a long visit.

A *ding* sounded at Fifteen. The ascent stopped, and the doors split. Durwood stepped off.

Clearing his throat, he walked the hall slapping doors with his palm. Whether they were lawyers' or bankers' rooms, vacant or occupied, he didn't know.

"You're dirty," he called. *"This deal is rigged, it's bogus— and I'll prove it. Game's up, ladies and gentlemen."*

Through the doors, Durwood heard stirring. Hushed exchanges. Deadbolts locking. Room service forks being dropped.

At the west end of the floor was room 1547. Above the printed number was a bronze placard that read: *The Chickasaw Suite.*

Durwood knocked.

He said, "Rudyard Raines, Sybil Fitzgerald—whoever's holed up in here. There's questions you need to answer."

He knocked for several seconds. Then he switched to banging, using the flat part of his fist.

A woman's voice: "Please leave—leave now. I'm quite certain this hotel does not allow solicitors."

"I'm no solicitor," Durwood said through the door. "I'm Durwood Oak Jones."

There was scrambling inside. He couldn't be sure, but it sounded like flapping sheets and scurrying feet over hardwood.

A minute went by.

"I'm still here," Durwood said.

Two minutes.

"Not going anywhere," he said. "Not until I ask my questions."

Eventually, Sybil Fitzgerald got the door.

Durwood had seen his share of snazzy hotel rooms during Third Chance missions. The all-glass suite in Reykjavík where Morfran Güice had aerified his death serum. Fabienne Rivard's spinning underground chamber in Monte Carlo where the remaining monarchs of Europe schemed to reassert dominion over the Continent.

He'd seen robot chefs, cryogenic safes, trapdoors made to look like Egyptian rugs. The whole nine yards.

The Chickasaw Suite was in that neighborhood. Chandelier twelve feet across. Plush divan. Canopy bed with a silk cover, folded under itself on one side. Laser net six inches below the ceiling, security of some sort. Painting with black and pink splotches that looked like an accident in the Valspar aisle of Home Depot.

"Stuffy in here," Durwood said.

The lawyer wore a skirt and rumpled dress shirt, no pantyhose. "We're in Texas. It's humid."

She gestured outside, where it had started raining.

Durwood eyed a digital panel on the wall. "Seems like there oughta be AC. Nice place like this."

He strode farther inside, ignoring Sybil Fitzgerald's

glare. A briefcase leaned against a spiral staircase, which led to a loft. Women's suits hung crooked over Louis XVI chairs. A shoe hid under the claw-foot whirlpool tub—freestanding on ivory tile.

"Let the record reflect you weren't invited in," Sybil Fitzgerald said. "My failure to immediately alert the authorities doesn't constitute consent to this unlawful intrusion."

Durwood ambled over to the bed.

Sybil Fitzgerald crossed her arms and said, "Ahem."

Durwood faced her. "Ma'am?"

She rolled her eyes at the formality. "You need to leave, Mr. Jones. Leave now and perhaps you'll sleep somewhere besides jail tonight."

Durwood raised his eyes to the chandelier. "Maybe I'll stay here. What's a room like this set you back?"

"The firm books at the monthly rate," Sybil Fitzgerald said. "Eight per night."

"Eight..."

"Hundred." She ran two fingers through her hair, which made one of its silver streaks disappear. "Quite reasonable compared to what clients pay to accommodate me in larger cities."

Hanging near the thermostat was a certificate bearing the Texas seal. Durwood read from it.

"'Hotel license granted to Raines Financial, LLC.'" He tapped his chin. "Interesting."

Sybil stood by the door. "The city had trouble finding local money. Rudyard stepped in to ensure this first-class facility got built."

"Real generous," Durwood said. "So you pay him eight hundred a night plus what your lackeys' rooms cost. Then you turn around, pass the bill right off to Hogan?"

The lawyer didn't answer.

Durwood circled the bed. Its canopy was fringed in velvet rope, hung with burnished brass buttons. His boot landed harder with each stride.

Sybil Fitzgerald whipped out her cell phone. "You've been given ample opportunity to vacate, Mr. Jones. I'm calling the police."

The closets. Heck, the place had a half dozen closets. Durwood approached the one closest to the bed. Its accordion doors didn't stand flush. Durwood tilted his head, like Sue-Ann coming up on a pheasant nest.

Except Sue kept her cool in such situations—and Durwood felt furious.

He gripped the curlicue handle and yanked the door off its track.

Chester Lyles stood among Sybil Fitzgerald's hanging clothes. Shirtless. Knees pinched together. He was handcuffed and wore a studded collar around his neck.

The chief operating officer of Hogan Consolidated screeched, "Get the hell away! You're trespassing!"

Durwood felt a thick physical revulsion. He turned from the sight and pointed to Sybil Fitzgerald's left ring finger.

"Don't put much stock in your vows, do you?"

She put her phone away with a snort. "My husband is the executive director of the American Red Cross. He spends forty weeks a year on the road, same as me."

"Hm," Durwood said. "Partners. Just like Hillary and ole Bill."

Chester Lyles hustled out of the closet over to his lover, red-faced. He held out his wrists for her to undo the cuffs. With contempt, the lawyer took a key from her pocket and freed him.

Lyles quickly dug up his own phone in a pair of slacks and made a call. "Damn it, Ozzie!" he roared. "How did he get up here? How'd you let him pass..."

Durwood said, "Were you aware Fitzgerald, Combs, and Doucey participated in lawsuits *against* Hogan Consolidated several years back?"

Lyles's face was too red already to make anything of.

Sybil Fitzgerald said, "My firm joins thousands of suits every year. This is nonsense."

"Is it?" Durwood turned to Chester. "Who came to who? Did y'all seek out Sybil's firm, or did she come to you?"

Chester didn't answer, busy pulling on clothes.

"Bet she came to you." Durwood turned toward the bed. "Bet she had a plan from the get-go."

Chester Lyles defended himself. "Jay Hogan—all the Hogans—they were asleep at the wheel! The company was getting trashed in the financial press. Valuations were in the crapper. Somebody had to take action. When Sybil approached us, it was a godsend."

Durwood looked to the lawyer. She'd slipped back into high heels, gained two more inches.

"No, sir," he said. "She sure wasn't sent by Him."

Outside, the patter of rain was steady.

Sybil Fitzgerald glared back, darker than a crow pecking guts out of roadkill. "You're wading into matters you have no ability to comprehend, Mr. Jones."

"No argument there," Durwood said. "But I figure I can find others who can. Folks in government. Reporters."

Chester Lyles jabbed a finger. "If this gets out, I'm suing you for every penny you're worth, you...*you thug*! I have a reputation! If anyone hears that you—er, that I—"

"This yours?" With his boot, Durwood picked up lace

panties from a jumble by the bed. "Don't leave your under-things behind now."

"Those aren't mine!" Chester Lyles said. "What do you think, I'm some...some kind of..."

"Yes," Durwood said. "I do."

Sybil Fitzgerald cut her eyes down yonder, saucy. *If those panties don't belong to Lyles, I guess she's feeling a breeze.*

Saucy or not, she wasn't playful with her next words. "This is a grave miscalculation on your part. Fitzgerald, Combs, and Doucey has done nothing extralegal here. Whatever cases you're referring to, they all took place out in the open, with free and full disclosure. What's to expose? It's all public record."

Durwood said, "There's disclosing on forms with some government clerk. Then there's folks taking a closer look, seeing the whole."

Sybil Fitzgerald spread her arms. "We're happy to wage that discussion in the court of public opinion. I have *teams* of messaging professionals ready to roll on my command."

Durwood felt his righteous energy—the feelings that'd spurred him up here, got him slapping doors—wane. Each word out of the lawyer's mouth chipped away at it. She was a step ahead at every turn.

Carol Bridges had said it: *Just because we're in the right doesn't mean we'll prevail.*

Durwood switched tactics. "Where you keep the files?"

The lawyer smirked, but not before something flickered in her eyes. They had moved, for a split second, toward the divan.

Divans usually had freestanding legs. Often bowed legs.

Not this one. This one's plush fabric was of a piece with the rest, had a wood skirt clear to the floor.

Durwood approached it. The bottom of the divan had no handles, but when he tapped it with his boot's toe, the sound was hollow.

Durwood tossed aside the furniture's throw pillows.

"Hey!" Chester Lyles said.

Reaching the bare top, Durwood stomped down hard. His bootheel fractured the wood easily and stopped at a box of files below.

The box was black.

Lyles said, "You can't look in there, those are our files. We have attorney-client privilege!"

Durwood reached inside the divan to pull out the box. He saw a second box—plain, uncolored.

Which did Gomez say was dirty?

Durwood thought it was the black. He started pulling the lid off that box when he felt hands on his shoulder. He twisted around.

It was the foreman.

Durwood kicked him four feet back, dropping the man into a sit against the bed.

The first folder was labeled *Billable Hours_Delaney*. Durwood removed a stack of documents and flipped through. His temples pulsed. Veins bulged in his forearms as he tried deciphering the figures. He couldn't make heads or tails.

Chester Lyles and Sybil Fitzgerald were shouting. Durwood tried shutting out their voices, willing himself to understand. Too much was pressing on him. Carol Bridges's warnings. Sue-Ann waiting back at the motel. Footnotes and clauses and too many damn words.

He squeezed his eyes shut. In the darkness, in the pounding of rain outside, his mind did clear. He remembered what he needed: evidence that Fitzgerald, Combs, and Doucey was behind these bogus personal injury lawsuits.

This was crossing lines. Several. Durwood told himself the evidence he'd find—even if it was just the overcharging—justified the means.

A riot of feet poured into the hotel room. At first, Durwood confused the noises with his own barbed thoughts. Then multiple hands were tearing him away from the divan.

There were eight: eight uniformed police. Durwood flinched away, spinning out of their grasp, crouched like a cornered cat.

Could he handle them, fight his way through? Likely he could. Durwood looked into their scared, angry faces.

No, he decided. The cost of escape was too great.

They were going to arrest him. He was going to jail.

CHAPTER THIRTEEN

Durwood was cuffed and taken from the hotel in a driving rain. One officer shoved him through the parking lot from behind. Another pushed his head down into the back seat, though Durwood wasn't resisting.

"Tough guy, beating up Ozzie," the one said. "They said he's in the hospital. You broke his spleen."

Durwood faced the patrol car's cage without talking. He couldn't buckle his seat belt in cuffs. Nobody buckled it for him.

He'd had a bum spleen himself, years back in Oslo. Never went to the hospital about it.

The second officer drove. The roads were deserted now, but the downpour sounded like rush hour. *Pit-pit-pit* on the cruiser's roof.

The talker said, "You're some kind of vigilante, right? Go around the country deciding who's right and wrong."

Durwood didn't think such a question needed answering, but the man spun and looked at Durwood around his headrest.

Durwood said, "I've put some miles on the van, seen a bit of the country. The deciding I leave to Him."

Chickasaw passed by out the window. Dark living rooms and watery streetlights. In the distance, a semi barreled across the plains.

The officers had closed the cage but neglected to lock it. Durwood could've looped his cuffs' chain in front of the passenger—the talker—and neutralized him against the steel bars. Then dived through the gap headfirst and speared the driver.

They would crash. If he timed it right, there wouldn't be much around to hit.

Durwood found comfort in these speculations. Other men played solitaire or did the Sunday crossword. He did this.

But no—he'd made enough rash mistakes for one day. He had been careless at the factory and allowed himself to be ambushed. He had intended to merely rattle Sybil Fitzgerald at the hotel; instead, he'd been distracted by her and Chester Lyles's perversions, and later been consumed by the files.

Now here he was under arrest.

The rain fell heavier still by the time they reached city hall and its basement jail. Durwood was marched up the front steps, socks soggy in his boots.

He saw a lone vehicle in the lot. A truck, but not the mayor's.

Inside, Durwood was handed off to the guard who'd checked him through security before.

The guard grabbed the chain of Durwood's cuffs. "Heard we had another coming for the hoot-scowl."

At a glance, the guard reminded Durwood of his

neighbor Crole. Face gray and grizzled, mouth full of rotten teeth. But where Crole usually wore an open, almost-goofy expression, this one pinched his brow to show he was a hard case.

The man signed several forms and took Durwood down to the cells.

"Working for the mayor, hm?" he said without looking back up the stairs. "You and the socialist."

The guard was bottom heavy and moved slowly. Durwood stopped often so his boots wouldn't trample the man's shoes.

The guard repeated, "I say, *You and the socialist, huh?*"

Durwood said, "I heard."

The jail had a dozen cells laid out on either side of a hall. The guard took a while finding keys, jingling his pockets, wheezing out his nose like he had more opinions to offer.

They stopped at a desk labeled *Receiving*.

"Me, I started with the other mayor," the guard said. "The mayor before. Fourteen good years."

Durwood waited.

The guard said, "He was better. Better leader, better ideas. Smarter. Guess he wasn't as good a politician as Carol Bridges. Your socialist buddy."

Durwood said, "Guess you know."

"I do." The guard finished signing a last form, pen just about poking through the page, and stood. "Bet that dusty hat'a yours I know." He squared his lumpy shoulders, measuring a fight.

There was a metal folding chair. Durwood sat.

Only one of the twelve cells was occupied. Naturally, the guard put Durwood there instead of giving him his own.

"You'll get along with this one." He nodded to Durwood's cellmate. "He's another loser. Blames Hogan for everything, all the world's troubles."

The words grated on Durwood, like bricks filling his head. He wanted to shut the guard up.

When he saw his cellmate, he felt even rottener.

Joad.

"They st-stopped me," he slurred. "They won't allow the truth to—er, to be exposed. And I *worked* in that factory, I did, two summers. It's not fair."

He spouted on about free speech and bloodstained factory bricks. His fingers kept doing and undoing the buttons of his plaid shirt.

Durwood sat on one of two steel cots.

"...fields of windmills and hemp, far as your eye can see! If anybody'd just open their eyes and *see*, and *imagine* a new Chickasaw..."

Joad tottered around a bare toilet as he talked, seeming invigorated to have an audience. He'd been picked up for trespassing or vandalism—the charges were unclear. He said his father had always preferred Chester. He said the South Texas art scene was derivative.

Durwood tried to ignore the words and focus instead on the cell. Concrete floor. Cinder-block walls. A barred egress window, which provided almost no light in the storm. The air felt stale—like a bass boat that never got scrubbed out.

Joad said, "Did you sniff out my brother yet, figure out the s-scam? I guarantee they're shorting labor somehow. That's how they *built* Hogan Consolidated—on the backs of labor."

His knee knocked into Durwood. Durwood moved.

The drunk kept on. "You look like a worker, you get it." He hiccuped. "Am I right?"

He dipped his head inquisitively, which threw off his balance. He stumbled.

Durwood caught the man by the elbow, though he'd have liked to let him fall.

"There's two cots, pick one." Durwood set the man upright. "I'll take the other."

Joad huffed and went back to the cot he'd been on before. The guard, out at his desk, laughed.

Durwood closed his eyes. His mood was as black as it'd been since arriving in Chickasaw. That he and this drunk, this weak excuse maker, were on the same side of things amplified his doubt.

Raines Financial would complete its deal for Hogan in forty hours. The documents were surely all drawn up. Press releases written. Rudyard Raines and Chester Lyles probably knew which wine they'd be toasting with for Friday dinner.

Durwood and Carol Bridges were a couple squirrels, chasing each other around the trunk of a sugar maple eight feet across.

It was late. Durwood tried sleeping, with little success. Joad woke to pee every half hour, moaning, scratching himself. He splattered outside the bowl and his urine stank.

The egress window was still predawn black when Durwood heard voices from the hall. He shifted onto his side to hear better—Joad snored and the rain hadn't let up.

"...nowhere in the protocol," Durwood heard the guard say. "Fourteen years and never, not *once* did Mayor Dix—"

Another voice cut in, "I don't care, Officer. There was plenty Mayor Dix didn't do during his tenure..."

The voice went in and out of Durwood's hearing. He caught what sounded like a sole on concrete. The scrape of chairs pushing back from a desk. Keys rustling. And then, finally, the approach of footsteps.

The guard waddled into view, every step slow and put-upon. It seemed like he'd never get to the cell. Likely he wouldn't have if not for the person walking behind, prodding him ahead.

Carol Bridges.

CHAPTER FOURTEEN

The guard sighed as he unlocked Durwood's cell. He sighed again when he relocked it after Durwood was out, then sighed more as he let Durwood and Mayor Bridges into an interrogation room up the hall.

"Thank you," Carol Bridges told him. "It's clear that was a great ordeal for you."

The guard stomped off, his mouth small.

The room had two chairs and a folding particleboard table. Durwood sat opposite the mayor.

She said, "You were going to be prudent."

Durwood smeared a hand across his eyes. "The situation deteriorated."

Leaving out the business about Chester Lyles and the studded collar, Durwood told her what had happened at the hotel. The foreman. The files in the divan.

Carol Bridges listened with a pained expression. "You forcibly seized their files?"

Durwood confirmed he had. Tried, anyhow.

"That was beyond reckless," she said. "You don't know

what was in those files, or wasn't in them."

"Some were black like your deputy said."

"Gomez *worships* you, Durwood. He could've told you anything to feel like part of the team. He could've made it up whole cloth!"

Her dark-red hair was damp. Maybe from the shower. Durwood hadn't seen a clock, but it must've been five, five thirty.

"I saw the files, I made a determination," he said. "Tell you what, though. Chester Lyles sure did jump when I went for 'em."

Carol Bridges exhaled toward the ceiling. "You can't substitute soldiers' intuition for due process. You simply can't."

Durwood's rough fingers dragged along the particleboard. "I need to get outta here. There's no time. Day and a half, this deal goes final."

"Don't look at me," the mayor said. "If I intervened, after what you did last night? My credibility would be shot."

"Credibility."

"Yes. Credibility." She leaned over the table, hot. "I've had to work for every ounce of respect I've received from the people of Chickasaw. They don't trust easy. They were wary of me at first, a Sooner transplant who thought she could govern this place."

"Where from in Oklahoma?"

"Gypsum Hills country," the mayor said. "Woodward. It was a little cattle town around the turn of the century."

"Great Western Cattle Trail, sure." Durwood remembered from old Miss Everly's class. "Seems to me you've done well for yourself."

"I have, Durwood." She was standing now, pacing. "As much as I like you, as much as I believe in you as a man, I can't just close my eyes and plunge in after you."

The woman's breaths were heavy and deep. Her passion filled the room, like certain four-star generals who'll walk into a barracks and change everything—change the air, change the smells. Turn the whole energy upside down.

Durwood liked her too.

He leaned close. "All I need," he said in a low voice, "is steel to get out that egress window. Steel nail file. Screwdriver. I'd take care of the rest."

Carol Bridges glanced over her shoulder. The guard was watching through the door glass.

"That's really beside the point—whether I get caught. I'm the mayor. The mayor doesn't break prisoners out of the town jail."

Durwood laced his knuckles. Her answer disappointed him on a tactical level, made it harder to stop these vile lawyers and bankers. On a personal level, he admired it. He felt that Carol Bridges was the woman he'd imagined three weeks ago when he'd first read her letter.

"Fair enough," he said. "So where's that put us?"

The mayor twisted her lips. She was standing in a stagger, tapping the floor with her front shoe. For several seconds, the noise was lonely, like a bullfrog's croak across a pond.

Then her cell phone chimed.

When Carol Bridges checked the screen, her eyes drew back into her head. Durwood had known the woman less than a day, but he felt her reaction viscerally: a gutshot.

"It's...it's from the hospital," she said, looking up. "Ozzie Jeffcoats just died."

CHAPTER FIFTEEN

Durwood Oak Jones had killed before. Many times, he hadn't known names or particulars, as in Iraq, or last fall dispatching the dozen-odd cult members trying to nuke their own Southeast Asian country to prove a point. These outcomes gave him no pause.

Other times, he'd killed to stop others from killing him. When it turned out the new clerk at Nethkins Feed & Fertilizer worked for the English mercenary Blake Leathersby, Durwood had deflected the woman's machete and sent her hurtling down the hundred-foot shaft of a grain elevator—and slept fine that night.

Occasionally, he questioned himself. Could he have saved the chief justice of the United States without putting a bullet through that phony court reporter's brain?

Had he used more C-4 than was strictly necessary to stop the zombie freighter bearing down on those geologists' lab in Vladivostok?

On hearing that Ozzie Jeffcoats—the foreman—was

dead, Durwood felt a chill inside. A pipe freezing some-where between his mouth and heart.

It quickly thawed.

He said, "I didn't kill the man."

Carol Bridges's face had turned a sick yellow shade. "I'm looking at the message." She turned her phone around for him. "It's from Deputy Gomez. 'I'm at the hospital, they just pronounced Ozzie dead of—'"

"I kicked him," Durwood interrupted. "Once. Men don't die from one kick."

"Unless the kick lands in the wrong place."

Durwood shook his head. "Who found him at the hotel? Who brought him in after this killer kick of mine?"

"Oh, one of the bankers. Name was something like Holmes."

"Holcomb?"

"Right. Holcomb."

Durwood remembered the pink-faced man with gym muscles. The room felt suddenly shrunken, like he could touch all four walls at once. He felt a prick in his palm—the particleboard had given him a splinter.

He reached across the table for Carol Bridges's hands. He looked her square. "My boot did not kill that man."

The mayor's fingertips were calloused like his. Maybe she built furniture in her spare time, or gardened barehanded.

"I want to believe you," she said, "but there was only one person in that hotel room wearing boots."

Durwood shook his head again, firm. "They're covering their tracks. I—I told that foreman something I shouldn't have. I told him about Sybil Fitzgerald's firm playing both sides of those lawsuits. He must've asked Chester Lyles about it."

"And then Chester Lyles...murdered him?"

"Well, Lyles or that Holcomb goon. One of 'em."

In this underground room, at an hour when most were asleep, Durwood knew his words sounded fantastical.

He said, "There's too much money at stake. It's down to the wire, they know it. They'll eliminate anybody who can expose them."

Carol Bridges tipped back in her chair. If Durwood was right, she was in danger too—though nothing in her posture suggested fear. He thought of the combat action ribbon in her office.

"I saw Ozzie myself just last night," she said. "I swung by the hospital before bed."

She looked thoughtful. Durwood kept quiet.

She resumed, "He wasn't critical. Doc Paisley mentioned the spleen. But, you know, I just felt like..."

"It's a spleen."

"Right," the mayor said. She almost smiled.

Clattering sounded up the hall, followed by voices. More than just the guard's.

How quickly had news of Ozzie Jeffcoat's death spread? Would the terms of Durwood's incarceration change? The nearest federal facility was Three Rivers, up by San Antonio, Durwood believed.

Carol Bridges must've been thinking along the same lines.

"They'll revoke your bail." She cut her eyes to the hall. "You'll get transferred. You won't get a hearing before midweek."

"After the deal closes." Durwood fixed his jaw. "By

then, Raines'll be auctioning off machines. Folks will have their walking papers."

There was more bustle from the hall. Carol Bridges stood and pulled both hands through her long, full hair. She paced. She looked out the door.

"No good, this is no good," she muttered. "They're coming. Looks like Dix's old attorney general, the creep." She braced herself by the table. "He's probably here to demand a transfer. Maybe I can stall, wrap 'em up in some red tape."

As she considered this, Durwood had the thought to go stand beside the door—back flat to the adjacent wall. When the guard and whoever else walked in, he could disarm them. Lock them in the cell with Crybaby Joad and beat it. Head back to the Sawyer House for those files. Show the whole world the truth about Hogan Consolidated's demise.

It was nearly breakfast time. If he went through with this omelet of a plan, he was going to break a mess of eggs.

"*No,*" Carol Bridges said.

Durwood turned both palms up. "What?"

"I can see what you're thinking. I can see, Durwood. But it can't be that way."

She had a way of saying his name. Her voice dipped there in the middle between *r* and *w*. It wasn't a growl, nor quite a grunt.

"Okay," he said. "What way's it need to be?"

"I have to take the lead. There are things I can do— within the confines of the law—to dig deep on Raines Financial."

"And the lawsuits. Don't forget the—"

"And the lawsuits," Carol Bridges said. "The files may be up in that hotel room, but those records exist other places. In those jurisdictions. I'll call around during business hours and get to the bottom of things."

Durwood felt a headache coming on.

"*Jurisdictions*," he said through gritted teeth. "*Business hours.* There's no time. No time for pussyfooting."

"This isn't pussyfooting!" Carol Bridges slapped the table. "This is called living with a realistic view of the world. It's called knowing you're not in some dime store shoot-'em-up, you can't just *ride the testosterone wave*"—she wobbled like she was on a surfboard—"from one fight to the next."

Durwood didn't answer. After her loud words, the room felt quiet.

Carol Bridges walked around the particleboard table, circling to his side. Her face was flushed from arguing. Her breasts heaved in her blouse.

"Stand," she ordered.

Durwood stood.

The mayor stepped very near. She took a long, appraising look at him. There was a stubborn kink in her forehead, and Durwood felt certain his own had a similar kink.

She raised one finger and held it aloft between his eyes. "If you let me down. If you can't contain the demons that live up here."

She pressed the tip of her finger into Durwood's hairline, the approximate center of his headache. The pain there diffused, or at least changed. He could smell her toothpaste. He could see the downy hairs of her neck.

Then, wildly, her hand was on his blue jeans.

On the back of his blue jeans. Her hand started from his belt and slid down—flat, urgent against his backside. The move brought their privates together. Durwood felt their heat mixing.

Her hand was in his back pocket, then out.

She backed away without expression.

In another second, the guard and a second man burst inside. Carol Bridges traded frosty words with them and left.

The guard made a snide comment to his new buddy, their eyes low on the mayor's body.

They came forward with cuffs. As Durwood offered his wrists, he was aware of an object in his jeans pocket. The size and weight felt about right for a pocketknife.

CHAPTER SIXTEEN

Durwood was led back to the cell. There wasn't much he could do to conceal the blade—if the object Carol Bridges had passed him was a blade. When his captors turned around, he swiveled so they wouldn't get a straight look at his pocket. Luckily they were too busy making taunts and insults to notice.

Behind bars again, Durwood was released from his cuffs. The door slammed shut behind him.

The rain continued vigorously, an everywhere thrum overhead. Before Durwood could sit, Joad—who'd slept through Carol Bridges—was up complaining.

"Is he my court-appointed lawyer?" Joad jabbed a finger at the new man. "I'd like a consultation now, now while the facts are fresh in my head."

The guard and the second man sniggered. The latter's unruly gray whiskers made Durwood think of a walrus.

Walrus said, "My days as a public defender are long done. Don't worry, they'll scrounge up some fresh graduate for you."

The response bewildered Joad. He yawned, wide and sudden. "Did I miss the boat on breakfast?"

The guard pointed out the window. "It's dark, bub. Go back to sleep."

Joad didn't have his wits about him. Taking this as a provocation, he said, "I will *not* go back to sleep. I know my rights, sir, and I am entitled to counsel. I am entitled to free and open speech like every citizen—"

"Cool your jets," Walrus said. "Minor charge, member of the Lyles clan? Mommy'll have you out of here by noon."

Joad began some huffy answer, but Durwood stopped listening. Stealing away to a shadowed corner, he slipped the object from his blue jeans pocket and onto the floor. It was a blade, sure enough. Nice one, twelve-in-one multi-tool. Leatherman. He placed it inside his boot.

Waiting for Joad to talk himself out, and for the lawmen to lose interest, Durwood felt a void. Some missing task or duty. He troubled several moments before realizing what it was.

Sue-Ann.

He hadn't walked or fed her. His internal clock must've kicked in—back home in Elk Garden, this was the hour he woke for such chores. The dog would be expecting break-fast. She was stuck in the motel, curled up on that stiff, scratchy carpet.

He resolved to see her soon.

Walrus had taken out his phone and was placing a call. Now he stalked the hall barking at whomever he had on the line. "Expedited" this, and "I certainly do have the author-ity" that.

After ten minutes, he jerked the phone down from his ear.

"The bitch threw up a roadblock with State," he told the guard. "She must've called in a favor." His whiskers twitched furiously. "But it won't last. She goes up the ladder, I'll just climb higher. Right over her"—he swore—"neck if I have to."

He glanced into the cell and caught Durwood listening.

"Don't think that lefty mayor's saving you," he called. "They're gonna love you over at Three Rivers, boy. Those thugs see a badass like you, their eyes light up. Chance to show everybody in the block what they're made of."

Durwood looked down at his knuckles.

Walrus told the guard he was heading home to catch a few hours of sleep. The governor's office didn't start answering its phone until nine anyhow. He'd call right then, explain they were sitting on a murderer, and have the transfer gift wrapped before lunch.

Joad gazed across the cell. "You killed somebody?"

Durwood returned to his cot and lay back, making like he intended to sleep more. "No."

Joad took a scared look around. "Because I—I wouldn't blame you. I know how entrenched these interests are. I realize what you're up against."

Durwood closed his eyes. As the rain pattered on, he thought. He had four hours until Walrus returned, but only one of the four—this first hour—would be dark.

He needed the dark.

A plan assembled in his mind. Durwood didn't believe Carol Bridges had given him the pocketknife with the intention it be used on people. This limited his options. He would have to favor stealth over force.

Settling on a course, Durwood lay quietly until Joad fell

asleep. His cellmate flopped over and back, and belched, and expelled snot in a farmer's blow. Finally, he dropped off.

The guard was snoring, too, by this time.

Durwood lowered one foot soundlessly into a boot. He removed the blade from the second boot and slipped it on too. Then he moved to the exterior wall.

The frame of the egress window started eight feet off the floor. Durwood could reach it on tiptoes—just. No chance he'd be able to gain enough leverage to pry open the thumb-lock mechanism.

The cell had no movable furnishings. The cots were bolted down. The toilet was plumbed into its pipe. To dislodge either would've woken half of Texas.

He'd have to scale the wall. The cinder blocks were joined by quarter-inch masonry grooves, which would have to do for toeholds.

Durwood wondered about the wall, whether it was structurally sound. Mildew streaks ran up and down, side to side. Clearly, the foundation had water damage.

What'd you expect, an escalator with handrails?

Hooking his fingers over the window frame as best he could, Durwood lodged the toe of his boot into the first masonry groove. Pebbles trickled to the floor.

Then he moved the second boot up to the groove, which made his backside stick out awkwardly. More pebbles fell. But Durwood stayed on the wall.

Groove by groove, he ascended. The higher he got off the floor, the better his grip got on the window frame. The fronts of his legs burned. His forearms trembled. His ragged breaths were loud—he fought to suppress them.

At last, he got high enough to prop his knee up onto the window frame. The other leg had nowhere to go, so he stuck it out sideways from the wall like some county-fair acrobat.

Now he could see the thumb-lock mechanism better. The design was typical, two matched tabs with a hollow in the top for your thumb.

But something was wrong with the tabs. There was a substance in between them. A clear substance.

He probed it with his fingernail, though he needn't have. He knew what it was: epoxy. And nothing so weak that Carol Bridges's blade would rupture it.

Dang it.

Durwood was exposed here, hanging half perpendicular off the wall. He cursed himself for not expecting the jailers to disable the thumb lock.

How else could he penetrate the window? Remove the glass pane? Disassemble the frame? Durwood had helped Crole demolish an old termite-ridden shed last week— those frames had eased right away from the studs. This wouldn't be so easy.

He squinted at the glass. Then he tapped and found it wasn't glass at all.

It was plastic. That Plexiglas junk they sold at Home Depot. The original glass had probably broken so many times, inmates throwing stuff up there, that they'd swapped it out.

The Plexiglas was fastened on the interior side. Durwood, after one look at those chintzy nails, knew this was the way to go.

He slipped the tip of Carol Bridges's blade into a large

edge bubble. The nearest two nails held at first. Durwood leaned into the pocketknife's handle, whose engraving read, *From your grunts—so you won't forget us when you're Madame President.* Durwood's tensed mouth relaxed in a momentary smile.

After ten seconds of steady pressure, the nails holding the Plexiglas sheared off. Not just the nearest two but that whole side of them.

Durwood worked the knifepoint under the Plexiglas's top edge next. He managed to separate it halfway before the nails got stubborn.

Working overhead, Durwood couldn't employ his weight as well. He considered scaling higher, but what would his boots hold on to?

He decided to slip through as the Plexiglas was, a side and a half dislodged. Plexiglas had some flex to it. He should be able to squeeze through to what he figured would be an outer trench running the building's perimeter.

Durwood wriggled his left arm outside and muscled that shoulder through the gap. The Plexiglas bulged, but not as much as he'd hoped. Maybe they shopped someplace different than Home Depot.

Still, he went ahead, wedging his head out next. The Plexiglas edge caught his scalp and gouged painfully—like a scythe trying to cleave his head in two.

Durwood could've backed up and tried to make a bigger gap. But every second meant more noise, more chances for Joad or the guard to wake up.

Durwood closed his mind against the sensation of tearing skin. He bulled forward. Inch by inch, his head moved. There was a noise like the Reichtor cousins back home ripping leather strips for those braided belts they sold at Nethkins. Warm blood trickled into Durwood's brow.

Finally, his head cleared the Plexiglas. The pane snapped hard against his back, but he'd gotten enough of his body through that now he was able to worm free.

In his determination, Durwood had completely forgotten the weather, and now plunged face-first into six inches of soggy mud.

The rain hadn't let up. Sludge filled Durwood's gums and eye corners. Raindrops pelted his bloody scalp. He went to push up, and all ten fingers sank into muck.

None of this troubled Durwood, who handled his own septic-tank issues on the farm. (He'd have sooner driven a Japanese car than pay another man to do the work.) Soaked to the skin, he looked up expecting a clear path to Main Street.

Instead, he saw a metal grate. Eighth-inch gauge cross-hatch, right above his head. If he'd have tried standing, he would've rung his own bell.

Durwood clenched one fist. The rain pummeled him—a thick, laughing torture.

He should've expected the grate too. He had judged the facility based on its keeper. He had seen a slow, dull man and without meaning to decided escape would be simple.

But the guard had nothing to do with decisions about thumb latches or grates. The guard hadn't decided a thing.

It was an old man's mistake.

Durwood flinched, and his left boot accidentally punched out the Plexiglas. It clattered to the cell floor below —not the sharp crash of glass breaking, but not quiet either.

He wasn't about to wait around and see whether Joad or the guard had heard.

Durwood looked up, eyes open to the rain, and fanned his hands across the grate. He ran his rough palms and finger pads along the crosshatch, feeling for imperfections. That mildew inside gave him hope.

Crabbing about on his knees, he slogged through ten yards of trench before feeling the right texture—scratchy, brittle.

Rust.

The ground outside city hall wasn't properly graded. Ten weeks out of the year, it probably stood in water like a Gulf Shore flamingo.

Durwood examined the damaged grate. Rust generally proliferates, spreading from a single point of weakness. So it did here. Two metal stretches connected to the initial spot bowed when Durwood pressed and led to an even larger patch of rust.

The distance between the two patches was about three feet. Plenty wide.

Durwood closed the pocketknife in one fist. In the other, he concentrated all the dissatisfaction he felt with himself. He staggered his stance, raising one knee and keeping the other lodged sturdily in the muck.

He punched up. The larger rust patch busted at once. The smaller held—resisting Durwood's stinging knuckles— but when he pushed the ruptured grate back that way, once, twice, a third time, it creaked and snapped.

Durwood pulled himself up through the new opening. Then he stood to his full height.

Chickasaw was asleep before him. Up Main Street, two lonely stoplights blinked red. Texas-12 was black in the distance. The rain poured over all with fresh, deadening intensity.

Durwood recognized the guard's double-wide truck in its former parking spot.

Two spots closer was a smaller truck: the mayor's. Smoke chugged from the exhaust. The passenger door was open.

CHAPTER SEVENTEEN

Durwood sprinted over soggy grass to Carol Bridges's truck. He tumbled into the passenger seat and slammed the door. The woman across the console was tired and tough and burning with intensity.

She pointed to the pocketknife. "Did you...?"

"Not a soul," Durwood said.

The humid air shimmered between them. Carol Bridges closed her eyes. A breath seemed to stop in her chest.

Is she having second thoughts? Does she figure she gambled the wrong way, seeing what a bloody mess I am?

Durwood thought she might switch off her motor and march him back to jail.

Instead, when Carol Bridges opened her eyes, she kissed him. Her knee was quickly over the console and between his thighs, then back.

"We have to go," she said. "Someplace no one can find us."

Durwood's lips buzzed, alive with her mouth.

He said, "Y-yes."

The mayor spun her tires, tearing out of the parking lot and up Main Street. Durwood's bearings took their sweet time returning. If he'd kissed a woman since Maybelle, he'd forgotten. He would not forget this. For a moment, he'd been lifted from the day's struggle—from his relentless quest for justice.

Near the outskirts of town, he spotted the motel and regained his sense.

"My dog," he said.

Carol Bridges raised her eyebrows. Whether amused or offended, Durwood couldn't tell.

She wheeled the truck into the gravel lot. Durwood's room key was back with the guard at city hall, but he'd left the window cracked. Now he slipped his fingers underneath the sill and lifted.

Sue-Ann's mottled nose appeared. She must've been up on her hind legs, a difficult thing with her bum hip. Durwood punched out the screen and lifted her through.

Sue-Ann rode in the truck bed beside a rod and a tackle box. Durwood didn't want the mayor's cab smelling like dog, and besides, the rain had let up.

She asked, "Do you have a phone?"

Durwood patted his empty pockets. "Nope. They took it."

The mayor drummed her steering wheel. "That's a problem. We're gonna need two."

She stopped at a twenty-four-hour convenience store out of town to buy a burner phone, then they drove a solid forty minutes in the same direction. The landscape changed from flat and bleak to wooded as they entered a forest of Spanish oak and what Durwood believed was black cherry.

The mayor handled her truck surely along banked turns

and over narrow bridges. The sun rose on Durwood's side, dappled through the tree trunks.

He caught sight of water at one clearing. After a series of switchbacks, a lake emerged. Durwood had dried out from his escape and welcomed the air's moist tinge now. His pulse slowed. His head wound had stopped bleeding—at the expense of half Carol Bridges's box of tissues. Closer to the banks, the vegetation grew lush.

Lush for Texas at least.

They veered off the road at a pair of unmarked ruts. The mayor powered them over a knot of roots and around a fallen trunk covered in moss, which had saplings growing up out of its decay. They reached a sandy stretch by the water.

Carol Bridges jammed the truck's gear stick to park.

"We're here," she said.

During the drive, they had settled on a course of action. Durwood's escape would be discovered soon, if not already. The mayor's midnight visit might arouse suspicion, but the rain should've erased her tire tracks—and thankfully the stingy city budget had never allowed for external cameras. So long as she made it back to her desk by ten o'clock, all would appear normal.

Before that, they needed to call the various jurisdictions where Hogan was facing personal injury lawsuits. They needed to know if Fitzgerald, Combs, and Doucey was behind the claims—like they'd been behind other spurious attempts to bring down the company.

The earliest these offices would begin answering their phones, in Carol Bridges's estimation, was nine o'clock. Which meant they had three hours to kill.

They stepped down from the cab and walked around to

meet in front of the bumper. Durwood's muscles throbbed, but it was a hearty, vital throb.

"You're taking a chance on me, I realize," he said. "I appreciate that."

His steel-gray eyes sought her browns. The brief embrace they'd shared earlier outside city hall bloomed now in the warm, free air. They took one another, staggering toward the lake, against a trunk, onto their backs in the sand.

Carol Bridges's body was firm and ready. They flung clothes into bushes and across the hood of her truck.

A doubt flashed into Durwood's mind, which was fevered and hardly working. A doubt about himself as a man—a man years out of practice. What did women today want or expect from these encounters? That naval investigator show he watched showed a steamy scene now and again but gave little wisdom.

Quaid Rafferty, who claimed wisdom on all topics relating to the fairer sex, said, "Women just want you to get lost with 'em. The chase is over, the masks are off. Follow her down until you can't spell your name."

Follow Durwood did. They rolled and clutched and felt and waited together. The lack of a bed—Nature's bed—seemed to suit them. The hollow of Carol Bridges's thigh gathered sweat and sand beautifully. Durwood gained purchase from the tough bark of a river birch.

After, leaning against Carol Bridges's body like one book against another on a shelf, Durwood recalled that he'd never helped Sue from the truck. Sheepishly, he went to check and found the dog sleeping, untroubled.

Nine o'clock snuck up faster than Durwood or the mayor wanted.

She took out the phones at quarter till. "Lawyers and document archives are the last things I feel like dealing with now."

Durwood, accepting the burner, tucked in his shirt and said, "Amen to that."

With the mayor needing to be back in Chickasaw by ten for appearances' sake, time was scarce. They decided to call in parallel, splitting the jurisdictions with cases pending against Hogan. Carol Bridges laid the list of municipal offices on her hood, set a rock on top to hold it against the wind, and dialed the first number.

Durwood dialed the second. He got a robot instead of a person, then he was confused by the menu prompts. Did he want "County Clerk's Office" or "Docket Schedule"?

He tried both. Both rang through to voice-mail recordings.

Durwood moved to the next number, which produced a similar result. So did his third, fourth, and fifth tries.

It was twenty minutes before either reached a live human.

"Yes, hi—*hi!*" Carol Bridges said, smacking Durwood's arm excitedly. "I'm calling in regards to a specific case. I have the reference number..." She read it. "Would you be able to provide a full roster of the defense attorneys registered in that complaint?"

She was standing on tiptoes, the strap of her bra twisted over one shoulder. Durwood fixed it.

Seconds later, her face sank.

"A formal request?" she said into the receiver. "I'm mayor of the city where Hogan is incorporated, and I'm requesting the information for official business. I imagine that makes it more or less formal."

The party on the other end gave some answer.

"No, I don't have access to a fax, we went digital," Carol Bridges said. "Fine. No...no, I need it much quicker than ten to fifteen business days... Of course, yes... I understand... And you, as well."

The mayor and Durwood faced each other grimly, holding phones at their sides like lumps of coal.

She noticed the time. "I have to go—I should've left five minutes ago."

Durwood shifted the rock to read the rest of the list. "Only two numbers left."

Carol Bridges winced, glancing back to the road.

"I'll take the last," she said. "It's that class-action suit, eight or nine injuries in a cluster. *Supposed* injuries."

Durwood tapped the number for the second-to-last case and put the phone to his ear. Three rising tones answered.

We're sorry, your call cannot be completed as dialed. Please try again...

He squeezed the phone until its plastic shell started crackling.

Carol Bridges blew out the side of her mouth, thumb hooked around her waist. She navigated a few prompts, and it seemed her call would end like Durwood's until a voice came through the line so bright even Durwood heard.

"Franklin Department of Judicial Records. With whom do I have the pleasure of speaking?"

"Carol Bridges!" The mayor knocked Durwood's arm again. "I'm a mayor—a mayor in Texas—and I have an urgent need to get the full list of defense counsel for a class-action lawsuit that happened in your jurisdiction."

"Oh!" the bright voice said. "Would you be referring to the Hogan case?"

"I would, yes!" Carol Bridges's fingers moved up and down Durwood's biceps. "My office is pulling together a, uh..." She snapped her fingers. "Honestly, it's busywork, the attorney general wants a review of legal proceedings he may get called into, and he's asking us to get this to him immediately—this morning, if you can believe it."

"I believe it," said the other over a keyboard's clacking. "Give me one sec, I'll pull it up here on my computer."

Carol Bridges poised her pen and flipped the list over so she could write on its back. The rock tumbled off her truck's hood.

Her expression was calm, studied, through the first three names she took down. When she heard the fourth, her grip tightened on the pen and she kicked sand triumphantly.

She wrote out *Fitzgerald, Combs, and Doucey* and circled it twice.

"And just—just while I have you on the horn," she continued, "the AG is also asking for contact info on plaintiffs. Would you happen to have phone numbers on those poor individuals who suffered injuries?"

Carol Bridges got those names and numbers too.

Capping her pen, she released Durwood's arm at last. She thanked the woman from Franklin profusely—"Bless your heart, this country needs a whole bunch more like you"—and ended the call.

She found her keys. "I have to hustle back to city hall. Can you call these people? Now they won't come out and admit fraud, but you should be able to get a sense. Just confirm our theory that the lawyers put them up to it."

Durwood squinted at the list of plaintiffs. The first name was *Rick Eichhorn*. "A sense?"

"A sense, yeah." Carol Bridges grinned. "Raise the topic, try to read their response. See if you can tap into their innermost feelings, Durwood."

As the ex-marine's eyes narrowed, she grinned wider and climbed up into the driver seat. She kicked over the motor and shifted into reverse—then froze.

She said out the window, "You don't have a thing to eat or drink here. And I have no idea how long I'll be." She hunted around her seat, moving aside a binder. "Sorry, I don't keep much clutter. If I had a granola bar or maybe a banana—"

Durwood lifted the fishing rod he'd noticed earlier from the truck bed. "Will you miss this, I borrow it for the day?"

Carol Bridges was still grinning. "I could spare it."

He examined the flywheel. It had no tangles. "Sue and I'll do fine."

"Take the tackle box too," she said. "Fish on that bait in the tin there, and you'll catch all you want."

Durwood took the box. "Stink?"

She nodded. "Make it myself with minnows, cherry Jell-O, beef lung, and Parmesan cheese. It carries a kick."

He lowered his nose. The smell was mighty, even with the tackle box buckled. "Ooh-whee. I'll say."

He ambled to the truck's door. They kissed through the open window, then Durwood watched her tires throw up dirt on their way back to Texas-12.

Sue-Ann slumped against his boot.

"There she goes," he said.

The dog looked up.

"What do you say, ole girl? Let's make some calls."

CHAPTER EIGHTEEN

Durwood Oak Jones was not a natural on the telephone. He didn't much care for his own, let alone this China-made burner. It felt like a toy, cheap, some funny shade of purple. He'd grown up with corded phones and had used steel walkie-talkies in the military. He didn't trust plastic to carry his words accurately.

Still, the job was the job.

He dialed the number Carol Bridges had written out for Rick Eichhorn. A woman answered, likely his wife.

"May I speak with a Mr. Rick Eichhorn?" Durwood said.

"I'm afraid you've missed him," the woman said. "He's at the specialist this morning."

"Specialist?"

"Yes, for his shoulder. We've driven all across Wyoming looking for one who can help."

Durwood stood with the phone at his ear, bootheels in the riverbank. He'd planned to say he represented the municipality of Chickasaw and needed to document victims of Hogan defects for official purposes. Which was more or less true.

"I'm sorry to hear that," he said. "Now, your husband—Rick is your husband, I take it?"

"Correct."

"Your husband's shoulder was injured when he fell off a ladder?"

"Yes, and that ladder's feet were on solid level ground," the woman said. "I popped those, uh, what do you call them? Hinges? I had them extended all the way. I know I did. But when he climbed up to that top step and tried looking over into the gutter, they gave out."

Durwood coughed. "The hinges?"

"Yes."

"And he, you say he was cleaning out your gutters?"

"Right. We have sweet gums all over the yard, hanging right over the house. Are you familiar with sweet gum trees?"

"My folks' property had several."

"Then you know," the woman said in her flat twang. "That sap's bad enough, but when they start dropping fruit? Them spiky brown balls?"

Durwood watched two dragonflies chasing each other through the reeds. "They can be a nuisance."

He spoke to the woman another five minutes. Durwood asked where the Eichhorns had found their lawyer, and the woman—she gave her name as Diane—explained they'd looked them up in the Yellow Pages. When he mentioned Fitzgerald, Combs, and Doucey, she first said she'd never heard of them.

"Wait," she said a moment later. "What was the name?"

Durwood repeated it.

"You know, it might've been on some form," she said. "I believe it was. They told us some bigger firm wanted in on the case, wanted to help. We signed a form about it. They had us sign about a million forms."

"Lawyers will do that."

As the call ended, Durwood's stomach felt hollow. The ground seemed to be rolling away from him. He looked up to orient himself and found the sun marching steadily up the sky.

Sue-Ann, sprawled out belly up, glanced at Durwood.

Next, he called the residence of Nancy Cortez. The line rang several times before there was an answer. Durwood nearly hung up.

"Hel-hello," a woman said, out of breath. "With whom am I speaking?"

"Durwood Oak Jones, ma'am."

"No kidding? I met a Durwood once," she said. "My apologies for the delay in picking up. I'm afraid I don't get around so well nowadays..."

Nancy Cortez, also, was legitimately injured.

Durwood reached three more plaintiffs. One had suffered nerve damage from hedge clippers built with Hogan parts. Another had broken his foot in a fall similar to Rick Eichhorn's.

The third was a big jerk. He barked at Durwood for calling him at home, said he was on the *do not call* list—both state and federal. Said people like Durwood were the scourge of society. *Wasn't four cracked ribs enough? How much longer would he have to endure the aftermath of this awful episode?*

You'd have thought he'd done three tours in Desert Storm.

But Durwood knew that jerks could get injured too, same as anybody.

CHAPTER NINETEEN

Carol Bridges called around noon. The news from Chickasaw wasn't good. An APB had been issued for Durwood. Federal marshals had been dispatched, and state troopers would be driving around with his picture taped to their dashboard. Durwood was to be considered armed and dangerous.

Fitzgerald, Combs, and Doucey had petitioned the city for more police at the Sawyer House on the grounds Durwood had tried stealing from Sybil Fitzgerald's suite once—and might again. The mayor had denied their request, but when she'd driven by later, several private security vehicles were parked outside.

Durwood said, "My news is worse."

He explained about Rick Eichhorn and the others injured by Hogan parts.

Carol Bridges said, "They could be lying. They could've been coached on what to say if anyone called asking questions."

Durwood shook his head. It took him a moment to remember they were on the phone—she couldn't see.

"They weren't coached," he said. "They got hurt. Hurt for real, all of them. Hogan's at fault."

"But that—but our *workers*," she pleaded. "I know what sort of workers we have in Chickasaw. I know their commitment to quality. This can't be."

Durwood understood her skepticism. He wouldn't have bought the stories either if he hadn't heard the pain over the line—the victims' winces, their wheezes. Their regret. People will do a lot for a dime. But they can't fake that.

He said, "We're sniffing up the wrong tree."

The mayor made a noise Durwood couldn't interpret. Then she promised to make it out to the lake later. Just now, city hall was crawling with law enforcement.

Durwood caught three bluegills for lunch. These were meager rations—Crole would've caught a barrelful in the same time. He kindled a fire with twigs and dried leaves, cooked the fish on a stick. Sue-Ann ate the heads but refused the tails.

Durwood wondered when he'd see Crole again. Would it be through plate glass, from prison? He thought about those letters he'd turned down in order to answer Carol Bridges's. The fired principal. Bad call in the Oregon State Little League championship. Something about a furnace warranty. How would those cases have gone?

Maybe better, but maybe not.

Durwood had made his own trouble here. He'd rolled into town with visions of cowboy law, imagined he was some blue-collar savior ready to give the moneymen the old one-two. Then he'd met Carol Bridges and her dark-red hair. Then villains in suits—Jay Hogan, Sybil Fitzgerald, Rudyard Raines looking like the Monopoly Man himself.

The story had looked simple, black lines on white paper. He'd nursed his own righteousness like the worst men of the age.

Durwood thought about Evie Sandecker-Lyles with one son in jail, the other likely in cahoots with people she despised. A woman who'd changed and adapted, and learned to accept shades of gray.

Durwood's rotten mood lasted the afternoon. He fished again and caught nothing, and in the bargain fouled his thumb and forefinger something awful with Carol Bridges's stink bait.

He napped. Napping should've been easy, poorly as he'd slept in his basement cell at city hall. But he squirmed and fussed in the heat, no matter how thick-canopied a tree he rested under.

His only small relief came walking Sue-Ann. Sue didn't take to exercise generally, but a walk now and again helped the hip. Arthritis is tricky that way. Today she ambled up in the middle of his doldrums, looking spryly up a riverbank path.

"Want to?" Durwood said.

She pointed and made a short whimper.

They walked twenty minutes. Sue's wind was decent— she even put a scare into a fat squirrel loading chestnuts into his cheeks. Durwood cracked a smile as El Tubbo scrambled into the brush.

Back where they'd started, Durwood slipped off his boots. He sat on a gnarled root. He felt lighter than before the walk but was mindful nothing had changed.

The mayor showed up around four thirty. Her truck

growled into view, throwing clouds of dust and reminding Durwood how peaceful the lake was without cars.

Carol Bridges stepped down from her cab. Her hip made a fine jut, but the strides were heavy and labored.

She explained, "I told Deputy Gomez I was leaving early for a spa treatment."

"He believed you?"

She shrugged. "I go every few months. The closest decent one's way out in Esperanza, so it buys me the rest of the day."

She leaned her backside into the truck's grill and sighed, looking like she'd rather be in Esperanza.

"I got a hold of your phone, briefly," she said. "They'd confiscated it for evidence."

Durwood said the burner was working fine.

"I know—I wasn't able to keep it," the mayor said. "I just wanted you to know there was a message. From your son."

Durwood looked up from the pebbles he'd been pushing around the dirt.

Carol Bridges continued, "He said he was worried. He said he was sorry he hadn't been more helpful before. Sounded like you two'd had a phone call?"

Durwood nodded.

"Well," she said, "he called. I thought you should know."

He met her eye in tacit gratitude. In the silence that followed, he wondered about Carol Bridges's own history. Whether it contained children or a marriage. Whether such a marriage would've ended in tragedy like his, or in some slower peacetime tragedy as most did.

It was hard to imagine this woman quibbling over bills

or who ought to take out the trash. Like Durwood's Third Chance partners, Quaid and Molly, Carol Bridges seemed born for big challenges.

Now she said, "If Hogan didn't gin up those lawsuits, then what happened?"

Durwood, returning to the present, said, "Hogan made defective parts. Plain and simple."

The mayor shook her head. "The Chickasaw workforce is one of the most competitive in the region. In the country. We invest in our people—in vocational training, in continuing education. These measures predate me, a lot of it Mayor Dix started. We designed our community around this function..."

She said more.

Durwood faced the lake. Sue-Ann was honking soundly in the grass, tired from her walk. The sun shone blood red through low branches.

At noon tomorrow, the sale of Hogan Consolidated to Raines Financial would be official. Eighteen hours.

The town would lose its largest employer. Rudyard Raines would gut the place, claim every write-off, sell every fixture—neat as a buzzard taking his sweet time with a carcass.

Carol Bridges said she'd spoken to the coroner. "Wayne Caldwell is a fair man, and I told him to check Ozzie's body thoroughly. They can't pin murder on you if his wounds are inconsistent—"

"I appreciate that," Durwood interrupted, "but you need to stop. It won't look good, you keep sticking up for me."

"Of course I'm going to stick up for you. I brought you

to Chickasaw. I wrote that letter to *Soldier of Fortune* in the first place."

Durwood said, "The town needs you."

"The town needs its leader to do what's right, to take responsibility." Carol Bridges tossed her hair, indignant. She was gathering steam. "If it all comes out—*when* it all comes out, what happened at city hall? I'll confess. I'll confess the escape was entirely my idea and resign my office."

Durwood said, "You'll do no such thing."

She glared at him. "This isn't your decision."

The air pulsed between them.

"No," he agreed. "It's not. But you're a smart woman, and smart women don't do dumb things."

There was no rekindling of romance after this. Besides the bluntness of Durwood's remark, there was this: they were wrong. No longer were they co-crusaders with the winds of justice blowing at their backs. They weren't Nancy Drew and the Hardy Boys. They were stuck in messy reality.

After a time, Durwood said, "The factory."

He said it almost unconsciously, the word dropping from his mouth.

Carol Bridges said, "What about the factory?"

"Whatever happened, wherever this thing ran off the rails," he said, measuring out his logic, "it started in the factory."

The mayor's eyes bored into Durwood. "You can't be suggesting going back to the factory."

He raised his brow.

"Back into town, into Chickasaw?" she said. "Where everybody and his brother's looking for you?"

He said, "Where did you think I'd go? Mexico?"

She smiled—unexpected, wonderful. "That rhymed. On top of all your other talents, you're a poet."

Durwood looked across the lake's mirror surface. He tried thinking up a phrase—another rhyme, some goof worthy of her joke. Nothing occurred to him.

"I've bent a hinge or two back into shape," he said instead. "I've seen 'em go bad. I got an idea what could have happened."

Carol Bridges stretched overhead and rubbed behind her own shoulder. "Will it do any good? What changes if you find a root cause? If these people's injuries are real..."

"I know," Durwood conceded. "But then we'd know. We'd know the truth."

CHAPTER TWENTY

Durwood would scout out the factory under cover of night, alone. With Raines Financial completing its purchase of Hogan tomorrow, Carol Bridges had a desk full of to-dos. Media requests, constituent emails, traffic planning for the noon ceremony on the marble steps of the Sawyer House.

"I was considering filing an injunction," she said. "If there's doubt about the legitimacy of these lawsuits, a court might block or delay the transaction."

Durwood advised her not to bother. "Lawyers, injunctions. It's enough."

They ate dinner out of nature, splitting a spotted bass she caught, plucking agarita berries straight from the bush into their mouths. They sat on a log. They passed a fork from her glove box back and forth.

Sue-Ann entertained them by hobbling into the water to her knees, then scampering out at the cold.

Carol Bridges laughed. "How old *is* that dog?"

Durwood drew back. "Figured you knew better than to ask that of a lady."

"Fair enough." She handed him the fork. "Have you spoken with your partners lately? Would they be...in range?"

Durwood had only sketched his Third Chance Enterprises backstory to the mayor. "Nah. Moll's got her kids. And I'm sure Quaid's sitting in hot water of his own somewhere."

"You don't want to get in touch, let them know where you are?"

Durwood scraped scales off a bite of fish and ate it.

They covered different topics waiting for the sun to set. Neither followed sports much, but Carol Bridges knew the linebacker from Durwood's West Virginia Mountaineers was having a fine season for the Cowboys. Durwood admired her necklace—its brown gemstone matched her eyes. She said it had been a gift from Aunt Jeannie and Uncle Don, who'd raised her.

Finally, it was time.

"I better ride in the footwell," Durwood said. "In case anybody pulls up alongside and gets curious."

Carol Bridges pushed the seats forward to give him space. Durwood packed himself in. Sue—who hadn't been mentioned in the APB or news reports—rode shotgun.

She shouldn't smell up the cab. That short coat dried quick.

The drive back into Chickasaw felt quicker than yesterday's drive out. Durwood had ridden transport to a thousand missions, and could recall few with a grimmer range of outcomes.

He needed to understand Hogan's failure, to see where

the men and machines had fallen down. The world was moving on from skilled manufacturing, fine. Durwood could accept that. What he couldn't accept was this Raines deal and its lack of accountability—like junking your old Chevy the day it quits without even popping the hood.

At a side street two klicks from the factory, Carol Bridges pulled over to the curb. She and Sue-Ann climbed out first.

"Thank you," Durwood said, accepting a hand up from the footwell.

Carol Bridges exhaled and looked him over. His boots, hat, everything in between. "Where will you go after?"

He looked down Main Street. "I suppose home."

"They impounded your van."

"Me and Sue have ridden Greyhound before."

The mayor hugged her elbows tight to her sides. "They can find you in Elk Garden."

"Who?"

"If you cross state lines, the FBI."

Despite the dire circumstances, Durwood's lips curled up. "We got places in the mountains, out east. Places won't show up on those boys' map."

His smile didn't catch to Carol Bridges. "What if somebody else wanted to find you?"

"Might be they could."

"Oh?"

Durwood removed the mayor's hands from her shivering elbows and threaded his fingers through hers. They kissed. Not fire and fury like before, but slowly. Durwood's arms wrapped her back, traveling it, seeking to cover every inch. Carol Bridges moved against him with fresh, frank hope.

When the kiss ended, she steadied herself by the truck. "Do you need anything?"

Durwood tapped the pocketknife still in his blue jeans. "Nope. Not so long as I can hang on to this."

"For now," she said.

"For now."

They parted, he and Sue-Ann starting for the factory.

They walked a mixed-use road that ran parallel to Main. Most commercial spaces were vacant. The residences were neat and modest, only a few cars rusting on blocks or bicycles left out.

The sight of the factory stirred Durwood. Factories always had. The pipes running up the outside of the building, the loading bays, the broad windows promising work inside—all these made his boots clap quicker over the sidewalk.

But there was more to his emotions today. There was shame today, embarrassment that the American worker needed subsidies and protections against foreign competition and still—*still*—made errors like those that had wrecked Rick Eichhorn's shoulder.

Durwood closed his mind to these thoughts. He wasn't one for grandiose themes. Leave that to Quaid Rafferty and folks on television.

The parking lot was empty except for a Camaro with T-tops somebody wanted twelve hundred dollars for. Durwood kept to an unlit aisle leading to the east side of the structure.

The entrance here was a regular door with a maglock. He hunted around the perimeter staying in shadow, gathering scraps. Receipts, deli tickets, empty ketchup packets.

When he had a fair-size stack, he began wedging items one by one between the door and jamb.

After the scraps had forced open a quarter-centimeter gap, separating the poles of the magnet, he tugged the knob. The door opened with no resistance. He and Sue-Ann slipped inside.

The factory floor was another two doors in. One was open. The other Durwood picked with Carol Bridges's pocketknife.

As he entered the assembly plant proper, his eyes instinctively rose to the ceiling. He'd visited yesterday but had been too busy deflecting blows to appreciate the facility. By the moonlight, it looked downright majestic. Stampers and presses, spot welders, conveyor treads—all giant scale. The grease smell Durwood loved as others love cinnamon and cloves in fall.

Sue-Ann loped off to sniff a closed door.

Durwood walked about until he located the riveter, a hefty slate-gray machine. He inspected the head, where an operator made adjustments in order to punch the proper rivet.

The orbital dial had Sharpie marks with alphanumeric labels, five or six. The metal was worn below where the chuck had been tightened.

Durwood removed the burner phone from his blue jeans to use for a flashlight. He peered at the wear patterns. Most showed clean, straight grooves.

Two didn't.

Durwood's pulse started pounding in his wrists.

The patterns below *LH* and *GH* weren't straight grooves. They had one prominent line and a second fainter one—a line of dimples almost.

LH.

Ladder hinge.

He wasn't sure of *GH*. Garden hinge? Maybe.

Somebody had moved the chuck from where it was supposed to be. They hadn't moved it often. Only rarely. Just enough to create a small number of large failures.

Who?

This kind of sabotage required knowledge of parts and machines—of Hogan's processes. Rudyard Raines and his desk jockeys couldn't have pulled it off themselves. They would've needed help.

A turncoat from Chickasaw.

Durwood stalked around until he turned up file cabinets. The whole bank of them was locked. Again, Durwood used the mayor's blade to open them—crudely, damaging the lock mechanism. He didn't care. This would not be a zero-footprint operation.

He rifled through folders, angling the burner's screen for light. He stopped at a master list of products and serial codes. Quickly, he identified which belonged to the defective parts.

It took longer to find the schedule of what had been made when. There wasn't a single schedule. He had to piece it together from printouts spread across a dozen different folders, one for each product family.

His head began throbbing. *Too many numbers.*

Durwood pushed through and completed the task, and now sought the one document he knew for certain he would understand: the visitor log. He found it in the first folder in the first drawer of the cabinet—like a wrapped box on Christmas.

He pulled out the logs corresponding to when bad parts

had been produced. Then, starting one calloused fingertip at the top, he scanned down the *Guest Name* column.

He kept seeing *B. Holcomb.*

Holcomb, he thought. *Holcomb, Holcomb...*

Then it came to him: the surname belonged to Rudyard Raines's right-hand man, Britt Holcomb. Mr. Gym Muscles, who'd tried pulverizing Durwood's hand at Boone's Chophouse.

When Durwood noticed that a second familiar name always appeared above Holcomb's, his head cocked sideways at first.

Then he laughed—he couldn't help it. A sad, understanding laugh.

Not wanting to put the cart before the horse, Durwood checked the discarded logs. Maybe Holcomb and his helper had visited the factory floor regularly. Maybe it was just coincidence they'd been around for the defects.

Durwood held the printouts against the cold concrete floor, scouring.

No. No—he didn't see either name in any other log. They'd only been present for the manufacture of LH and GH parts.

All Durwood's use of the burner as a flashlight had run down its battery, but there was enough for a call. He tapped Carol Bridges's number and waited for her to answer.

"*Durwood.*" Relief gushed through the mayor's voice. "It's you. Great. Tell me you're not in custody."

"I'm not in custody," he said. "I'm at the factory, and I know. I know what happened."

He told her to bring Deputy Gomez, and her chief of police, and if she knew anybody with a newspaper byline, to bring them too.

"Why, what did you find?" Carol Bridges asked.

Durwood had a snap panic about Sue-Ann's where-abouts, then he found her still sniffing that closed door.

"Proof," he said. "Proof that what happened here wasn't fair."

CHAPTER TWENTY-ONE

In the thrill of discovery, Durwood had not thought deeply about the deed perpetrated by Britt Holcomb and his enabler. Now, as he waited for Carol Bridges, it sank in. The cunning. The ruthlessness. Sending death traps rolling off the assembly line because there was money in it.

Durwood paced a tight circle to nowhere. The headache those numbers had given him intensified. Profiteering was nothing new. Durwood expected profiteering, understood a certain amount was inevitable—even healthy—for a thriving economy.

But profiteering here, in a factory like they'd done? Putting blame on workers, turning it back against them to take their jobs?

Talk about kicking folks when they were down.

There was a line of hard hats on pegs. Durwood slammed them openhanded, knocking several to the floor. One clattered to rest in his path. He kicked it.

A clipboard sat in a plastic caddy, likely containing safety or productivity measurements. Durwood punched the caddy dead center. The clipboard and its data splintered to shards.

He grabbed up the logs, the folders, the mapping of products to serial numbers. He stuffed it all into a trash bin.

Sue-Ann whimpered.

"Ah, I know it's dumb," Durwood said. "I know it doesn't change a thing."

The documents should be preserved for evidence, he knew. Well, he could get them from the bin later.

Sue whimpered again.

"I told y'I know," he said. "Now be quiet!"

But the dog wasn't responding to him—to his behavior. She was still sniffing at the closed door.

Durwood dropped his chin to his chest. He allowed his heart to slow before walking through the disarray to Sue's door.

The dog sat.

"Think something's inside?"

Her milky eyes shifted to the door, then to Durwood, then back.

He twisted the knob and pulled.

It was a janitor closet. Mop bucket. Paper towels. Jugs of cleaning supplies. The supplies must've caught her nose.

"Happy now?"

Sue-Ann poked into the closet to investigate. Typically Durwood wouldn't have allowed this, but he found no will now to correct the animal.

He returned to the front of the factory to wait.

How long had it been since he'd spoken to Carol Bridges? Fifteen minutes? Twenty? He didn't know where she lived, how long a drive it was.

Carol Bridges. Now that he'd burned off a little of his

own gas, he had a moment to consider what tonight meant in her regard. They'd been vindicated. There were still ruts to bump over, but Hogan Consolidated would be saved. The logs, forensic analysis of the chuck—it would be enough, even if they never found a soul who'd testify.

The mayor would receive credit. She'd deserve it.

How would she respond? Likely other opportunities would arise. Would she choose to stay in Chickasaw, keep a good thing going?

Or pursue another thing—good too, but different?

Finally, a roll gate's *clack-clack-clack* sounded from the side.

Durwood moved toward the noise, his heart plump in his chest. When the loading bay's door finished opening, Carol Bridges was there.

She had people with her, but not the right ones.

CHAPTER TWENTY-TWO

The whole gang of crooks was there. Sybil Fitzgerald stood back a piece with two of her yes men and Chester Lyles. Rudyard Raines tapped his paunch in the shadows. And up front, Britt Holcomb pushed Carol Bridges ahead by a fistful of shirt.

Her wrists were bound, and a rag was stuffed in her mouth. A cut at her temple was bleeding.

Raines called through the dim factory, "Whatever it is you think you've found, we'll be happy to take it off your hands."

Durwood cursed his own stupidity. Getting distracted, wallowing first in rage, then wispy thoughts of Carol Bridges. He'd let down his guard. He should've been watching from a superior angle, perched in a high window monitoring the mayor's approach.

It might not have been enough to save her. But it would've beat this.

"Found?" Durwood repeated. "How do you mean?"

The banker looked at Sybil Fitzgerald with a fat grin. They laughed.

"A good liar you're not," the lawyer said. "I don't believe professional diplomacy is in your future. Better keep your day job as..." She rolled her tongue around her mouth. "Whatever your day job is."

Carol Bridges was bucking against Britt Holcomb's grip, trying to speak around her gag. Holcomb jerked her aside and made her red hair whip.

Durwood said, "Fella, your hands need to come off that woman. Now."

"Or *what*, you—" Holcomb used a slur. "Think you're all country strong. Think you're bad, huh? Come on, get some of this."

Still holding the mayor with one arm, he flexed the other bicep and kissed the muscle's peak.

"Enough, Britt," Rudyard Raines said. To Durwood: "Let's dispense with the bluffs, shall we, Mr. Jones? We heard every word you said to the mayor."

Sybil Fitzgerald muttered, "Precious few there are."

Durwood scanned their number, counting, calculating. "You had her phone bugged."

Raines neither confirmed nor denied. He ambled to the fore past Holcomb and Carol Bridges.

"You said you knew what happened." He turned sideways as he talked, looked like a Bartlett off one of Grandma Jones's pear trees. "Said you had proof."

Now it was Durwood's turn to neither confirm nor deny.

"Factory made bad parts," he said. "Folks got hurt. Pretty cut and dried."

A disbelieving smile went around the other side.

Durwood wasn't fooling anyone, he knew. He needed time to make a plan. Sybil Fitzgerald's yes men were both armed, as was Britt Holcomb. So three guns, six hostiles altogether.

Or was it five?

Durwood had seen Chester Lyles two times: cool and collected at Boone's Chophouse, then furiously embarrassed in his kink partner's hotel room. He was someplace in between now. His tanned skin had a green tint, and his hair looked dented.

Had he taken a step away from Sybil's yes men?

Durwood had put Chester Lyles into the *villain* camp after finding him in that closet. Now that he knew the details of the scam, though, Durwood thought again.

What if Chester Lyles hadn't known about the factory sabotage? What if he'd taken Hogan's liability at face value and thought selling out was their only option?

Sybil Fitzgerald said, "Rudyard, we need to hustle. Somebody could drive by and see cars. We need to contain this. Keep it tidy."

"So we do," the banker agreed.

He focused his gaze—two pinpoints set back in deep sockets—on Durwood. "The visitor logs. That's what you found, the visitor logs. Correct?"

Durwood kept his face as straight as he could.

But Raines said, "Yes, you did. I can see it, you most certainly did. The question is where—whether you moved them."

He dispatched one of Sybil Fitzgerald's men to check the file cabinet. The man returned after a minute and said the logs were gone.

Raines smirked. "Of course they are. Mr. Jones has taken

private property—private records, like those he attempted to steal from the Sawyer House. And now we must reclaim them." He unrolled one arm formally. "If you'd be so kind, Mr. Jones, please show us where you've hidden the files."

"Wouldn't," Durwood said.

"Excuse me?"

"I wouldn't be so kind."

Rudyard Raines frowned, hitching his thumbs through suspender loops. As he darkly considered Carol Bridges and her captor, Holcomb, Durwood raced through scenarios.

He felt certain Raines and Fitzgerald—with Chester Lyles's participation or not—planned to kill him and Carol Bridges. They would need it to look like an accident or murder-suicide. Durwood was officially a fugitive from justice; they could make it seem like she'd been trying to apprehend him.

Maybe they planned to burn the place to the foundation and only wanted to be sure Durwood hadn't stashed the files off-site.

"You're right," Durwood spoke up. "I found 'em. I found the stinking logs."

Without meaning to, he singled out Holcomb with his eyes. Holcomb—whose name had been one of those in the logs. Who'd moved the riveter's chuck and doomed those people to their injuries.

"You're angry," Raines observed. "That's because you don't understand multimillion-dollar deals. These deals are finicky. Market conditions have to be right. Hogan Consolidated needed to go down, like a parched forest or some firetrap in a crowded block of wooden houses. We just" —he gazed around the high reaches of the factory—"helped it on its way."

As Raines gabbed, Carol Bridges—stooped under Britt Holcomb's grip—pinched her eyes at Durwood. She was trying to communicate something. She kept glancing down, then back at Holcomb, then down again.

Put him...what, on the ground?

Bury him?

She ducked her head twice. She bulged her eyes urgently.

Durwood puzzled at her attempted clues. He studied the ground beneath his boots. *Is there some advantage in the concrete?* Years back, he'd sprung Quaid Rafferty from a similar standoff—on the ridge of a giant hydroelectric dam under a madman's control—using the current underfoot.

But the juice here wasn't on.

Then Durwood realized she didn't mean the ground. She meant her hands.

He looked more closely and saw that her wrists weren't actually bound. They looked bound, but they weren't. She was holding them together for show, but the zip tie was broken. She was holding it in place between her palms.

The understanding must've shown in his face—she gave half a smile and motioned again to Holcomb.

She can take out Holcomb.

That was good. That helped. Two against five (or six) was better than one against six. A bit.

"Chop-chop, Rudyard," Sybil Fitzgerald cut in. "We're not smoking brisket at Smitty's here."

Rudyard chortled. To Durwood and the mayor: "I didn't want this project, but Sybil sold me on the merits of Texas barbecue. She was right. I'd lived a sheltered life in Manhattan."

Sybil, taking an ironic bow, snatched a pistol from her yes men and pressed it into Carol Bridges's head. "Tell us where the lousy logs are. Tell us now or your girl gets it."

Durwood started at the sight of the muzzle against the mayor's ear.

"Don't!" Fitzgerald pressed the gun harder. "One inch closer, and I swear I'll blow this Reba McEntire retread to the Rio Grande."

Durwood stopped.

The lawyer said over her shoulder, "Tonight goes onto your bill at hazard pay, Chet. Base times ten."

Chester Lyles stood back and bit the corner of his lip.

Durwood shook his head, disgusted. He observed, "She forgot to bring your collar."

"Oh, spare us all the antiquated moral compass," Fitzgerald said. "It's tired. *I'm* tired. And you, Mr. Marlboro Man, are out of time."

Her finger poised on the trigger. She spread her feet.

Chester Lyles said, "But what—what're you doing?"

Rudyard Raines looked uncertain too.

Sybil Fitzgerald said, "Let's just shoot her and burn the damn place. Right? It's easier. The files are here. They're paper. Paper burns."

She closed one eye and seemed on the verge of firing.

"Wait!" Durwood said. "Don't shoot, I'll tell you where the files are. I will. I'll tell you."

He made a lowering motion with one hand, as though gentling the factory air. When Sybil Fitzgerald did take the pistol away from Carol Bridges's head, Durwood felt like his body had been freed from a vise.

Fitzgerald said, "Where."

Durwood flicked his head left. "There."

The lawyer growled and re-gripped her gun. "Where *precisely*?"

Durwood raised his hands. "Hey, okay. Settle down, I'll tell. I'll be as precise as I can." He breathed deeply and prayed. "I put the logs in the janitor's closet."

CHAPTER TWENTY-THREE

Sybil Fitzgerald handed her gun back to the yes men.

"I still prefer petitions and pretrial motions," she said, smoothing out her blazer, "but that felt nice. I could get used to packing heat."

She started toward the janitor's closet, heels clacking. The door was leaning shut.

Durwood had gotten Sue-Ann from a breeder down in Buckhannon. Her ma and pa were both blueticks with good hip genes. Go figure. Pa had one white ear, which wasn't in the breed standard, but Sue and her littermates came out regular.

She took instruction well enough coming up. She gave Durwood few problems. Wasn't a chewer. Rarely growled. Durwood's method for correcting puppies was to lift them, rear end high, then drive them fast toward the ground, pulling up at the last. Dogs don't like it nor do they quickly forget. Sue only got this treatment once.

Still, Durwood had owned dogs that minded better. Shepherd, a black lab he'd owned in the service, could hold his stay for an afternoon. Another bluetick, Pearl, would fetch Durwood's *Coal Valley Times* every day before making her first water.

In this situation, though, there was no dog Durwood would've rather had behind that door than Sue-Ann.

Sue had a knack for mischief. At picnics, she would play possum until everyone left their plates to throw beanbags, then she'd climb up a bench to polish off the potato salad. If you were sitting someplace she wanted for herself, she'd slide in next to you, nudging, nudging. Bit by bit, she'd move you off the spot.

These proclivities often paid off during missions. Like the time she tripped the fail-safe switch on the nuclear sub in Dudinka, with Durwood trapped in solid ice. Or befriended the cannibal's daughter in Kuala Lumpur and got her to disarm the ground-tunneling missile seconds before it hit the earth's molten core.

Quaid Rafferty swore she could read and write—if only she'd had one hand in place of a paw. "Better than either one of us, Wood. I honestly believe that."

Now Durwood watched the janitor's closet door, contemplating a second prayer. The door was heavy gauge and opened outward to a dim area shadowed by a catwalk overhead.

To the left, Carol Bridges was still under Britt Holcomb's control. She flexed her hand in place and looked ready for action.

When Sybil Fitzgerald got close, Durwood stole two quiet strides toward Rudyard Raines. He peeked at the man's waist and pockets to confirm he was unarmed.

Rudyard leaned away. "I like my personal space, hombre."

Durwood glanced down his body. "Sure got plenty of it."

The banker beckoned to Britt Holcomb, maybe for help. Before the overpumped errand boy could respond, Sybil Fitzgerald was opening the closet.

A blur of mottled black-and-white swarmed the lawyer, knocking her to the concrete floor. Sue's teeth clamped on to the woman's blazer. Her paws stomped and gnashed. Sybil Fitzgerald whipped her head back and forth, shrieking.

At the same time, Carol Bridges slammed an elbow in Britt Holcomb's gut. He *oofed* and fell. She dropped to a knee, slugged his face, and took his gun.

Durwood bulled into Rudyard Raines. His head hit the banker's sternum, and he tucked his arms into the man's paunch, holding him like a blocking dummy between himself and the yes men.

"Help me, damn it!" Raines shouted. "Shoot him —*shoot!*"

The yes men wagged their gun barrels around.

"But we can't," one said. "It's gonna hit you if I shoot, it's gonna..."

He spluttered out. He was used to pushing paper around an office, not dealing with hostage situations.

Durwood kept bulling Raines forward, cutting down their angle. The yes men's eyes quavered. They lowered their guns and raised them. Then lowered them again.

When Durwood got close, he shoved Rudyard Raines and knocked one yes-man over like the ninepin in a bowling split. He and the banker tumbled together into a heap.

Durwood tackled the other.

Meanwhile, Carol Bridges had Britt Holcomb in hand. Sue-Ann's teeth were still clamped on Sybil Fitzgerald's blazer.

Fitzgerald said, "*Somebody get this flea-bitten piece of*"—she unleashed a string of curses that would've made a merchant marine blush—"right now, you idiots, *now!*"

But the yes men were unavailable, one pinned by Durwood's boot, the other underneath Rudyard Raines. Carol Bridges had an uncharitable grip on Holcomb's arm.

The only one of her gang available was Chester Lyles. A gun lay at his feet. It had clattered away when Durwood tackled the yes-man.

Rudyard Raines managed to sit up.

"Get the gun, Lyles!" he huffed. "Pick it up *now!*"

Hogan's chief operating officer looked at the gun, but his eyes were unfocused.

Durwood said, "Kick it over to me. It's not too late to do right."

Chester Lyles's foot moved.

"For your town," Durwood urged. "For Chickasaw."

The whole room was watching Lyles. Even Sue, standing on top of Sybil Fitzgerald, cut her milky eyes that way.

The young man's expression was complex. First he was looking at the riveting machine. Then at Rudyard Raines, his partner in negotiations.

Was he angry, thinking about the sabotage? About being forced into bad terms by those injuries and lawsuits?

Or was the sabotage not news at all? Was he thinking damage control, how best to sweep his own involvement under the rug?

Maybe he wondered how Durwood and Carol Bridges would treat him if he switched sides this late in the game.

The mayor must've been wondering the same.

"I'll pardon you," she said. "The city won't press charges against you personally for anything. You walk out scot-free, free as a bird."

Chester's face lightened. "You—you'd put that in writing?"

From underneath Sue-Ann's paws, Sybil Fitzgerald snapped, "She's lying, Chester, you moron. The mayor of Bumblefrick, Texas, has no authority over the state. Over federal charges."

Chester turned back to green.

Sybil continued in a venomous bedroom voice, *"You've followed me this far.* You keep following. I am your master and you *will obey."*

Durwood was so stunned by the lawyer's transformation—horns could've risen from her head and surprised him less—that he said nothing. Carol Bridges was also slow to counter.

Chester Lyles picked up the gun and walked it to the yes-man. The yes-man used it to cover Durwood and the mayor.

Rudyard Raines grinned—a gloating, savoring grin. Sybil Fitzgerald tried standing in triumph, but Sue's stiff paw stopped her.

"Call your damn dog," Sybil said. "Get it off me *now."*

Durwood did nothing.

She ordered her man, "Make him do something about this filthy mutt."

The yes-man centered Durwood in his sights, squinting down the barrel.

Hard to say if he had it in him to fire. To take Durwood's life. Men can be cowardly ten times in a row and find their fangs on eleven.

Chester Lyles clenched and unclenched his fists. Maybe he regretted his choice. Maybe in the moment, his lover had hoodwinked him with mind control—Molly McGill could've said.

Didn't matter now. He was ten feet away and unarmed.

"Sue," Durwood called sharply, and whistled.

The dog sat bolt upright on Sybil Fitzgerald's throat. Then gave Durwood a doggy smile.

"No," he said warningly. "G'on, girl. Let her up."

He twitched his middle finger. Sue loped off, limping on her bad side.

The lawyer stood and spit repeatedly. "Eck—fur tastes like my grandfather's cigar case." To her side: "Okay, time to set this train back on the rails. We can still make the noon presser, though nobody's getting any beauty sleep."

She rearranged her chess pieces. Rudyard Raines untangled from the one yes-man. Durwood released the other. Britt Holcomb gripped the gruff of Carol Bridges's neck as they switched spots—but let go when Durwood flinched at him, and resumed holding her shirt.

Again, Durwood stood isolated on the factory floor.

Now what?

Sue-Ann was sleeping against the drill press. There'd be no more tricks up her sleeve.

Durwood's body was battered, and felt it. The gash in his scalp from the Plexiglas had opened, blood trickling through his hair into the grooves behind his ears.

The factory seemed to be watching, listening. Judging every last one of them.

The lights came on.

"*What?*" Sybil Fitzgerald snapped. "What in the—?"

The yes-man zipped his gun around, aiming it around the newly bright factory.

Durwood checked the drill press. Sue-Ann was slumped against the base, snoring.

Somebody else was on the loose.

CHAPTER TWENTY-FOUR

After the lights, the machines came on. Conveyors creaked alive. Stampers pounded empty molds, one *bang* after another. Ventilation ducts started sucking, a high whinny that set the air moving.

Rudyard Raines's face curdled like he was listening to awful music. Sybil Fitzgerald plugged her ears.

Durwood caught Carol Bridges's eye. He found the mechanical noises tolerable, even soothing. The mayor—a combat veteran herself—didn't seem to mind either.

The racket got even louder when the riveter got into the act. Next came the pneumatic press. *Toink, toink, toink...* A symphony of metal, gears, grease, and motion.

Sybil Fitzgerald barked to her yes men, "Cut the juice— go find the power. Some timer must've kicked in. Give me your gun, I'll keep them in line."

The yes men did as they were told, and left.

Durwood reassessed the situation. Now there were four hostiles in the immediate theater: Sybil, Rudyard Raines, Britt Holcomb, and Chester Lyles—the wild card. And facing those four, two friendlies. Three if you counted Sue. The numbers were improving.

A minute passed. Sybil Fitzgerald checked her phone.

"I don't like this," she said. "They should be back. How long's it take to flip a switch?"

Rudyard Raines asked, "Does anyone else know we're here?"

The lawyer slid one hand down her hip, considering.

Durwood didn't believe a timer or switch was at play. The factory was operating below capacity. Hogan didn't need to run a third shift. As far as motion detectors, any of them would've gone off long ago.

No, it must be a person. Security guard? Policeman who got curious, passing in his cruiser? Either of these could be helpful—unless they happened to be in the lawyers' or bankers' pocket.

There was a startled cry above. Loud grunting. Foot-steps—or foot stomps—echoing through the factory. A blunt noise that could've been a fist hitting a jaw.

Then: "Argh*hhh*."

Rudyard Raines shot Sybil Fitzgerald a withering look, seeming to question her men's competence.

The noise above continued. Sharp words, then another anguished groan. Then more footsteps—closer. Durwood looked up to the catwalk that spanned the factory's upper reaches. Somebody was up there.

The somebody passed into the light.

Deputy Gomez.

"Freeze and surrender your weapon!" he shouted, aiming his own at Sybil Fitzgerald.

Though Durwood was a fair distance below, he thought he saw a smile behind the deputy's frantic expression.

Sybil Fitzgerald didn't lower her gun. "What did you do with my men?"

"Your men are disabled." Deputy Gomez's weight shifted from foot to foot. His barrel was moving too much. "I saw you kidnap the mayor from city hall. I—I saw, so I followed."

He eyed the lawyer. The lawyer eyed him. The machines kept chugging. The catwalk above trembled—could've been its supports were leaning against a machine. Or the deputy's shaking knees.

Carol Bridges shouted, "Gomez, *fire! Take her out!*"

The deputy looked between the two women. "She'll kill you."

"Doesn't matter," the mayor said. "The truth needs to come out. Stop her and get the evidence, take it to the FBI."

He said, "Evidence?"

The mayor looked to Durwood. He realized she didn't know herself. All he'd said over the phone was that he had proof something hadn't been fair.

Durwood nodded to Britt Holcomb. "Fella here moved the chuck on the riveter. He sabotaged it, caused the defects that hurt those people."

Rudyard Raines cleared his throat and accused Durwood of having "a fanciful imagination indeed." Sybil Fitzgerald chimed in, bragging her firm would've nailed Hogan Consolidated eventually—with or without the defects. They'd been looking at other legal remedies. Accounting abnormalities. Incomplete SEC filings. When a white-shoe firm like Fitzgerald, Combs, and Doucey put an organization in their crosshairs, it was only a matter of time before they succumbed...

Wrapped up in her own talk, the lawyer didn't notice

Carol Bridges beginning to creep. The mayor stayed in the same line of sight but backed toward the shadows. She moved with knees bent, inch by inch. When Sybil Fitzgerald did glance over, she would lean forward and appear not to have moved.

But she was moving.

Rudyard Raines gestured dismissively at Gomez. "He's a nobody, he won't shoot. Let's get on with this fire. Chester, go fetch the gas cans from the truck."

Lyles obeyed, slinking out through the delivery bay.

The banker threw back his shoulders as if saying, *There we are, finally a bit of progress.*

Carol Bridges was creeping again, halfway to the shadows. With Lyles gone, though, one fewer body in the factory, her movements were more noticeable. The next time Raines or Sybil Fitzgerald looked, they might see it.

Durwood needed to be a distraction.

"Y'all are, uh, not getting away with this," he said.

The lawyer and banker scoffed to each other.

Once, as they'd been waiting for an Azerbaijani scientist to finish synthesizing the first ever element of the periodic table's eighth row, Quaid Rafferty had called Durwood "a conversationalist on par with cabinetry." Durwood hadn't argued. He fared poorly when talking just to talk. Every useless word felt like some tiny roofing nail you'd spilled and had to go hunting through the grass for.

Rudyard Raines said, "Fire has a way of eliminating loose ends, I'm told."

"Well," Durwood said, stalling. "Even fires leave trails."

"Perhaps." Raines winked and added, "I like our chances with the Chickasaw Fire Department on the case."

Out the corner of his eyes, Durwood saw Carol Bridges scowl.

"Hogan's in the news, this big deal of yours," Durwood said. "Now there's a fire in the headquarters and factory? Bet the FBI wants a peek."

Rudyard Raines explained that his ties to the federal government ran long, long and deep.

As the argument continued, Carol Bridges made steady progress. Shimmying backward, her kneecaps low and shifty. Any sounds were covered by the factory bustle.

Still, she needed time.

Durwood asked Sybil Fitzgerald, "You enjoy destroying these towns like Chickasaw? Is it money, hundred percent, or you do it for the sport?"

The lawyer fondled her gun handle. "These little towns," she sneered. "These people do it to themselves. You can always find somebody to turn. Somebody ready to stab his neighbors in the back."

"Like Chester, your boy toy?"

She chuckled. "What can I say, we do our homework. Chester needed instruction after Daddy left. He needed a firm female hand, an anti-figure to his tree-hugger mother."

Durwood shook his head, marveling. "You're something else." He gestured to Raines. "Guess that makes big man here your pimp."

Fitzgerald swung her gun wildly. "*I* run this show. Who do you think ordered your beating when you went sniffing around Jay Hogan? When Chester came whimpering into my room. *Whatever will we do? Bridges brought in some guy, some cowboy-investigator, oh no!*"

"I see he isn't back yet," Durwood said. "With the gas. Maybe he's running."

"He won't run. He wouldn't dream of defying me."

Durwood traced a line in the concrete with his heel. "Could be you aren't as good as you think." He looked up from the line. "In the sack."

The lawyer laughed, slow, lusty. "You're pathetic. You're begging for it, aren't you? All these repressed years of faux righteousness. You'd just love a modern woman to come rip those tight jeans off you and—"

As her talk became vile, Durwood checked Carol Bridges's progress. She was nearly safe, within lunging distance of the shadows. He looked next to the catwalk. Deputy Gomez had his gun poised.

Durwood's eyes gave the smallest uptick.

Gomez fired. Sybil Fitzgerald crumpled to one side— he'd clipped her thigh. She pulled her own trigger on the way down, but Carol Bridges had rolled away behind a conveyor belt. Bullets *pinged* around the factory.

Durwood sprang forward, planting both hands on the concrete and whipping his boots in a sidewinder kick that sent Rudyard Raines sprawling.

Britt Holcomb spun around looking for Carol Bridges, but she stayed out of sight behind the conveyor. He turned, instead, to face Durwood.

Durwood stood and faced him back.

Deputy Gomez shouted from above, "Stand down *now*! I have you in my sights, *stand down now!*"

Holcomb ignored this. He began circling toward Durwood.

"I'll send you back to the rodeo, clown," he said. "Yeah, clown. You know I will."

Durwood countered each of Holcomb's steps with an opposite step of his own.

"Stand down!" Gomez repeated. "I said *stand down now!*"

The deputy came pounding down the rickety catwalk stairs. Durwood felt each step in his molars. The impacts echoed off the machinery—erratic, abrasive. Gomez's approach seemed too loud, though Durwood couldn't have said how else he might've gotten down.

"Step away *immediately!*" the deputy warned. "That's Durwood Oak Jones and he's a national—"

Deputy Gomez never got to say what sort of national thing Durwood was, because another blast sounded as he reached the last step.

The deputy tumbled into the railing, bleeding from his shoulder. Twenty yards away, Sybil Fitzgerald lay wincing on her side over a smoking muzzle.

"Alonso!" Carol Bridges cried.

The mayor scampered away from cover and dove onto the woman who'd shot her deputy. They struggled on the concrete. The gun skittered away like rocks over a frozen pond. Sybil Fitzgerald thrust knees, fists, fingernails at Carol Bridges. The mayor kept calm and reversed each attack, pinning the lawyer's limbs one at a time until the woman was subdued.

Rudyard Raines was still on his back from Durwood's kick, moaning. He was holding his heel. Likely he'd severed his Achilles.

Britt Holcomb slapped his own chest with one hand, then the other. "You and me, clown. Time to get down and dirty."

Durwood tracked the man's showy approach. Holcomb made a quick spooky face. He feinted, then he laughed at Durwood for twitching.

When Durwood spent the energy to move, he moved with purpose. His boots traveled short paths to their next spot. He kept balance. The muscles of his arms readied. All around, machines methodically carried and shaped and polished invisible products.

Holcomb drove his foot forward in a stomp. Durwood gave ground.

"Back on your heels," the younger man said. "I see you. I see you scared, punk *bitch*."

Durwood moved them with a sidestep, cutting off the other's angle of escape.

Holcomb's footwork was recognizable. He might've trained at a boxing or mixed martial arts gym. Maybe he got his language there too.

Durwood glanced away at Carol Bridges, who was tearing strips from her own clothes to bind Sybil Fitzgerald. The lawyer wasn't making it easy. She kept working a knee or knuckle free.

To their left, Deputy Gomez lay on the ground. He looked pale.

Taking advantage of Durwood's distraction, Britt Holcomb attacked. He plowed into the ex-marine's solar plexus. Durwood lost his wind, feeling his boots lifted off the ground. With Holcomb's growl in his ear, they tumbled to the floor.

The nearby riveter's impacts throbbed in Durwood's cheek. He fought to shed Holcomb's weight, but the man was a load—twisting, raging.

Their faces were inches apart. Holcomb gritted his straight white teeth, his eyes ghoulish.

Straining, Durwood worked his knee loose and thrust it into his attacker's thigh. Holcomb covered the pain with both hands, allowing Durwood to slip through a straight right.

Holcomb flew off but was up in a flash.

Durwood got up too. They squared off in the same poses as before, both worse off by several cuts and bruises.

There are moments in battle when you bide your time and let the fight develop, and others when you trust your own savagery.

Now was time for savagery.

Durwood ran at Holcomb. The man wobbled at the sudden aggression. He tried slamming his joined fists down upon his adversary's head, but Durwood was already in his kitchen.

Durwood's momentum picked Holcomb six inches off the ground, then he slammed the bigger man down onto his side. He drew up his boot to target Holcomb's face and end the encounter, but then—hesitating—decided to kick the stomach instead.

That split second gave Holcomb his chance. He caught Durwood's boot in his hands and twisted viciously, bringing Durwood down.

As he crashed, Durwood's knee felt like Grandma Jones's Thanksgiving turkey getting one of its drummies twisted off.

Holcomb struggled to all fours. He loomed over Durwood.

"Better call that dog of yours," he said. "Get him to bail you out again."

"Her," Durwood said.

Holcomb's face squeezed. "Huh?"

"Her, she," Durwood said. "My dog's female."

Holcomb was sizing up a punch. Durwood gripped his injured knee and writhed around—more than necessary.

"What your dog's gonna be is dead," Holcomb said. "Dead like you."

As he drew back his fist, the factory itself pulsed through Durwood's body. Its heft and heart and steady, unexciting rhythms. Carol Bridges was watching across the floor. Deputy Gomez was wheezing, possibly hanging on to life.

Durwood grasped his knee and winced, pushing his chin forward. Making a target of it.

Holcomb tucked his thumb into four red fingers and swung.

Durwood spun away at the last moment. Holcomb's knuckles exploded against the factory concrete. He roared in pain.

"Aaah! Jeez, I—oh, I broke it," he said. "I'll kill you!"

But Durwood had already crawled around on his one good knee and locked him up in a half nelson. Holcomb bucked against the hold, headbutting Durwood in the mouth. Durwood's grip faltered. Holcomb pistoned back to ram his torso into Durwood's.

Durwood crabbed backward to absorb the blow, managing to regain his grip.

He squeezed Holcomb's neck, in control. "Are you done?"

Holcomb bucked again and whipped his head up and down.

Durwood, keeping the half nelson, used his other fist to punch the man's spine.

"Good 'nuff?" he said.

Holcomb didn't answer.

Durwood punched his spine again. Harder. He heard Carol Bridges's voice in his periphery.

He said, "Good 'nuff?"

Holcomb, on his knees, was sinking like a slab of butter left out overnight. He mumbled something.

"What's that?" Durwood demanded.

Holcomb tried mumbling again. "I'm...okay...I'm—I'm done."

Durwood released the man. He fell to the concrete.

With effort, one leg unable to bear weight, Durwood rose to his feet. He stood tall in the middle of the factory. Bloody. Battered. He allowed the industrial noise to wash his wounds, the solvent and grease smells to be his balm.

His mind rose above bodily suffering to consider the fate of this stubborn, ugly place. It would continue—this ugly work. In ten years, there might be nothing but robots here. It might be every last thing got made in China or Thailand or the next place up.

For now, though, Hogan Consolidated was going to live. And its workers were going to work.

CHAPTER TWENTY-FIVE

T he next day was all questions. The FBI set up shop at city hall and did their debriefs. *Who brought the guns? Who fired first? How did the factory machines start running? How many hostiles? What happened to the last one?* Nobody had seen Chester Lyles since he'd left to fetch Rudyard Raines his gas cans.

Durwood got tired fast of repeating himself, of the whole bureaucratic kit and caboodle.

Did this G-man, pen wagging off his thumb like grasshopper wings, really need to hear again what exact verbal warning Deputy Gomez had given Sybil Fitzgerald before firing his gun?

"I explained all this," he told his fourth agent in two hours. "Fella before you had a notepad, maybe he'd lend it to you. Let you make a copy."

Between interviews, Durwood was taken to a waiting room. The local paper—special afternoon edition—sat in a jumble of magazines and announced in bold type, *Hogan Sale Stopped Amid Accusations of Fraud, Sabotage!* over pictures of Rudyard Raines in handcuffs and a walking boot, and Sybil Fitzgerald stabbing a finger in the air.

Durwood had crossed paths with Carol Bridges here in the waiting room a few times. She'd puffed her cheeks. The feds must have been giving her the same treatment.

They had spoken little. After the standoff, they'd sat guarding the culprits until the authorities showed up. Words hadn't seemed right then—in front of others, after such violence. Then the doctors had kept her in the hospital overnight.

Durwood thought he might see the mayor again now, in the waiting room, but he didn't. He decided to leave before another stooge took him away to ask all the same questions. He'd been officially exonerated in the killing of Ozzie Jeffcoats—the coroner had found fibers tying the fatal wound to Britt Holcomb. He was a free man. If the FBI had more questions, they could find him.

Durwood walked outside into the thick Texas air. Peaceful Beans was buzzing, customers streaming in and out by the front door.

Durwood headed to the counter. He ordered coffee, though it was late in the day.

Evelyn Sandecker-Lyles broke away from her partner to greet him. "Here comes the man of the hour! Make way, everybody."

Durwood shrugged off "hoorays" and hearty pats on the back.

"Gomez deserves that honor," he said of the deputy, who was in stable condition at Chickasaw General. "And it's a woman did most of the heavy lifting."

"It usually is." Evie gestured around the cafe, which was standing room only with workers, retirees, kids. The whole town. "We're all waiting for her to get out. I've got a petition going to rename Main Street as Carol Bridges Way."

"No kidding." Durwood accepted a clipboard and added his signature. "Bet you dollars to donuts she vetoes it."

Evie tipped back her head and laughed.

Through the sea of bodies, Durwood spotted his former cellmate, Joad, in a corner. He was sipping from a mug and keeping to himself. It looked like he'd cleaned up some, combed his hair.

Murmurs started from the front of the cafe. Durwood left off considering Joad and turned to find the source of the commotion.

Jay Hogan was coming his way.

"Thank you, Mr. Oak Jones," the CEO called over the crowd. "On my family's behalf, on this town's behalf"—raising his voice grandly—"thank you for saving our company from those vultures."

Durwood considered the hand before him, blue-veined, delicate. He did shake it. "They're vultures now, are they?"

The young executive seemed to be expecting the challenge.

"I was blindsided!" he said. "All the information I received suggested we had to sell, there was no alternative. Chester screwed up. Chester gave me rotten—"

"Stop," Evie interrupted. "I won't allow you to denigrate my son here. You can keep talking, keep sticking your silver foot farther into your mouth. But do it someplace else."

Three men in work bibs started showing Jay Hogan the door.

He flinched out of their grip. "Why is Chester still missing? Did you ask yourself that? Why's he a fugitive, why haven't they found him? I'll tell you. Because he's ashamed. It's obvious he was involved in the scam."

"It's not obvious to me," Evie said.

Hogan whirled toward Durwood. "You're the one who unraveled the mystery—tell her. Tell her there's no way those outsiders could've sabotaged those parts without help from somebody who knew the factory."

Durwood straightened his hat. "I believe they were helped."

Hogan and Evie Sandecker-Lyles both waited for him to say more.

Durwood sipped his coffee.

A man in a frayed trucker hat stood from the counter, yawning. He bellowed, "Aw, now we gotta go back to work. Thought I might be looking at some vacation."

But he was grinning, celebration in his voice. The crowd cheered.

Jay Hogan patted the man's burly shoulder. The worker pulled away like the CEO's touch was bird scat on a park bench.

Evie remarked, "You should resign, Jay."

Hogan reared back. "That's ridiculous. I just came up against some bad actors, bad circumstances. I didn't intend any of this to happen. I'm not responsible."

"Yes, you are. You were negligent."

Jay Hogan refuted the claim, and Evie suggested if he didn't relinquish control of the company, folks in town might sue for damages. Her partner, Nina, tried tempering her, touching her elbow, but several in the crowd took up the argument. Some joined on Evie's side, others Hogan's.

Around and around.

Listening, Durwood felt sour. He didn't consider Jay Hogan much of a businessman, nor care for the idea of him continuing to lead the company. But he liked Evie's idea of litigating the matter even less.

He, Carol Bridges, and Deputy Gomez had saved Chickasaw from lawyers and investment bankers. Would the town fritter it away?

Maybe Sybil Fitzgerald was right. Maybe they'd just end up doing it to themselves.

The squabbling was enough to make Durwood wish for Quaid Rafferty's company. The last time they'd spoken, his partner had been fired up about a sidehustle he had going with Greenpeace—something to do with red panda habitats. He'd talked an hour before Durwood said he needed to get on the tractor and handle some chores.

Durwood's mind was just drifting back to West Virginia, fond thoughts of sorghum and fishing with Crole, when a police cruiser pulled up outside Peaceful Beans.

The officer called from the door, "Horace Lyles?"

There was confusion. Most in town knew Horace Lyles as Evie's former husband, the man who'd flown the coop to Belize.

Durwood looked to the corner where Joad was.

Evie cried, "What—what is this?"

The police officer walked inside. "I have an arrest warrant for Horace Lyles Jr. on multiple counts of criminal sabotage with intent to harm others."

Joad, over the heads of the whiplashed crowd, said he'd never intended harm. "They slashed the quality control workforce! Those defects should've been caught—it was meant to highlight the greediness of the layoffs, the recklessness." He looked to his mother, whose upper lip was quivering. "But who—er, I mean, I dunno what Holcomb said, but—"

"Holcomb didn't say a word," Durwood cut in. "I'm the one who told. I saw your name in the logs."

Joad's eyes skittered between his devastated mother and others in the crowd. "It—it was supposed to affect *change*. The exploitation has to stop! It has to—I just wanted it to stop!"

As the officer dragged him away, Evie leaned over her sun-worn forearms on the counter. Customers and friends muttered sympathies. Nina rubbed her back.

"*Two sons*," she said, her voice aching. "Two sons I've lost to that place now. That company."

Durwood approached the counter.

"Children are hard," he said. "They're all we make of them. Till they aren't."

He thought of Cade, in the ground at Arlington Memorial Cemetery, who'd embodied his and Maybelle's values but had been impetuous. He thought, too, of Luke up in New York City, who seemed at times to belong to a different species.

Evie continued to sob. Townsfolk crowded around her, tired, healing.

Durwood set his mug by the register.

"Miss," he said to Nina. "Could I trouble you for a paper cup? I'm taking my coffee on the road."

CHAPTER TWENTY-SIX

The Vanagon picked up a noise around Grayson. Durwood figured it was a bad belt, maybe that serpentine that seemed to wear out quick on Volkswagens. By Roanoke, though, the noise had developed a crunching quality. He pulled off I-79 to an auto-parts store, rolled his sleeves, and crawled underneath.

The brake rotor was striking metal on metal. Durwood bought a twenty-dollar pad and was back on the road in a jiff.

He'd meant to push through tonight but, after the delay, decided to find a motel. He'd started the drive dead tired, after all. He didn't trust his eyelids to stay open.

He slept four hours.

Late morning, he pulled into Elk Garden. The weather was clear and warming as the van rolled up his gravel drive.

"Dang, that johnsongrass," he said to Sue-Ann. "Figured it'd be up some, two days. Not like this."

Durwood stepped from the van and stretched. His neck,

what felt like his neck anyhow, cracked. He pulled the sliding door open, but Sue's chin stayed put on her paws. She'd been gimpy since her tussle with Sybil Fitzgerald.

"C'on, girl," he said. "We're home. Bet your old rabbit friends missed you."

As he waited on the dog, Durwood's steel-gray eyes swept the farm. Whenever he returned from an absence, he saw chores. The split rail needed a coat of paint. The barn had a few cedar planks that looked ready to fall next time a nor'easter blew through.

More trees were leafing out, though the big red maple near the house was still taking its time. He stepped closer and saw the bark looked worse than before. That ring of divots from the yellow-bellied sapsucker had grown.

His gaze moved up the tree, along its leftward fork, until he saw the big squirrel's nest. It had a new gash in one side—looked like something had plucked out several twigs.

Something like a yellow-bellied sapsucker.

Footsteps lumbered over gravel behind Durwood. He turned to find Crole, holding a jug in the crook of his finger.

His neighbor flashed a rot-toothed grin and said, "Look what the cat dragged in."

They embraced. Sue-Ann, seeing a familiar face, forgot her injuries and hopped down to greet Crole too.

They went inside. Crole toasted Durwood with a shot of moonshine. He tried getting Durwood to reciprocate, but the Jolly Rancher stench turned the ex-marine's stomach.

"More for me." Crole wiped his mouth. "So. Seems y'all made out okay down in Chickasaw."

The *Coal Valley Times*' reporting was similar to the Chickasaw paper's. Further details of the plot had emerged in the last twenty-four hours, including Horace "Joad"

Lyles's role in the parts' sabotage: the unholy alliance he'd made with Raines Financial, hoping to advance his agenda. It was widely speculated that Chester—still missing—had served as a go-between. Durwood doubted this, knowing as he did the truth of the brothers' relationship.

Prosecutors had started tallying up the staggering fees Hogan had paid its predatory partners, cataloging the conflicts of interest. Watchdog groups were already calling on attorney generals across the country to examine the cozy relationships between top law firms and Wall Street banks, the professionals who oversaw—and profited handsomely from—these region-shattering deals.

Durwood told his neighbor, "I need to make a call. Meet at the spot, say another hour?"

Crole hoisted his jug and stood. "An hour, you bet. Give those fishies a reprieve."

On his way out, he rubbed Sue's ear between two fingers.

Durwood took a few minutes gathering himself. He unpacked his suitcase and ran a wet rag over the card table and baseboards, which had gathered dust. Then he called Luke.

They'd spoken once since the ordeal. Luke had been emotional, offering to fly down immediately, his shaky voice reaching through the phone. Durwood had assured him there was no need.

Now Luke's voice sounded normal. "You made it, hey. The old van-o-war didn't break down on you?"

Durwood smiled. *Van-o-war.*

"Just once," he said. "How are you? Did that IPO issue come out alright?"

"What's that? Oh—the IPO we were working. Yeah,

yeah, we delivered," Luke said. "Feels like forever ago. Actually, everybody here at Goldman's talking about you. How bizarre is that?"

"Me?"

"You're making waves, Dad. You started a movement."

"We stopped a crime," Durwood said. "I don't see where it's a movement."

"No—it is, Dad. It really is. You're the talk of the Street."

Durwood shook his head, imagining stockbrokers looking out their hundredth-story windows and discussing Chickasaw, Texas.

Luke said, "The guys have been ribbing me, saying it's bad for business. None of our new issues are gonna get approved."

"I hope you're able to do what you need to," Durwood said.

"It's fine," Luke said. "Honestly, these deals need to get looked at. Firms like us, we're supposed to walk behind picking up crumbs on these transactions. Not swing hammers and *make* the crumbs fall."

Durwood walked with his phone to the screen porch. Morning had given way to muggy midday. He needed a shower.

He asked if Luke had Thanksgiving plans.

"Not especially," Luke said.

"Remember how your mother used to cook the yams?" Durwood pivoted on one bootheel. "Candied with a little nutmeg. Boy. You and your brother could put down a plateful of those."

Luke clucked at the memory. "Didn't she grow them?"

"The yams? Sure. Here in the garden, I'm staring at the spot now."

"That's great," Luke said. "Great, good stuff."

He went on to say he'd probably do Thanksgiving with this girl he was seeing. They might skip the turkey, though—she was vegan. Maybe they'd find a restaurant. An Asian fusion place had just opened down the block. The online reviews he'd read were incredible.

Durwood said, "Noodles, that sort of thing?"

"Right, Dad. Noodles."

Durwood watched the far-off Appalachians, holding his son's voice in his head.

"Enjoy it," he said. "That's something to be thankful for, a good woman in your life."

After a pause, Luke said yep, it sure was. Keyboard *clacks* sounded in the background.

Next, Durwood walked out to the spot. He found himself considering Chester Lyles. Was he holed up in Mexico? Or Central America? Would he try contacting his mother, who was suffering through her second broken heart?

Durwood hoped he would sometime, whether he'd been part of the sabotage or not. The Lyles family had plenty of years yet. Their legacy contained good that shouldn't die with the sins of one generation.

Crole was already fishing.

Durwood, taking the next rock over, began stringing his bait caster. "They biting?"

"Just started," Crole said.

Durwood gave the ten-cent version of his Texas adventure. Jay Hogan. The ambush. The foreman's death. Escaping jail with the mayor's pocketknife and hiding out at the lake, overcoming Britt Holcomb at the factory. Finally,

Joad's reckoning and his own doubts about the town's ultimate fate.

Crole sipped liberally from his jug throughout the tale.

"That mayor," he said with a moonshine warble. "I saw her on the nightly news. Didn't I?"

"She's been on."

"You and her turned back some powerful foes."

Durwood smiled, watching his line in the gray river.

Crole said, "Look like the sort a man could spend some time with."

He glanced at Durwood. When his neighbor didn't meet his eye, Crole squinted into his jug like it had things swimming around inside, which it might have.

"That's so," Durwood said.

He was thinking of her pocketknife, that he ought to have thanked her properly. For the blade. For believing in him.

He ought to have told her he'd enjoyed their afternoon at the lake.

Back with Crole, Durwood reeled in his line and sent another cast soaring toward the horizon.

Plunk, landed the lure.

He asked, "What's new here? River looked high coming in."

Crole made a face like he was deciding whether to let the change of subject stand.

"We got rain yesterday, good rain," he said. "I had a four-inch swimming pool in my crawlspace."

"Fix your gutters," Durwood said. "Every last one of those downspouts is plugged."

Crole took another swig. "I know. Been waiting for you to come over and do it for me."

They fished an hour for bluegill, Crole using woolly buggers, Durwood live crickets. Sue-Ann watched from the banks. The men hooked a dozen between them, the larger share belonging to Crole.

Next, they fished trout on an assortment of spinners and rooster tails. The sun climbed high overhead. Durwood laid out his swollen knee across a rock. Crole went too hard at the jug and gave himself a nosebleed.

"Ah, enough with these guppies," Crole said after catching three juvenile trout. "Let's take a run at old Walter."

Walter was a legend of the Hatfield-McCoy region of the state, a blue catfish said to weigh north of two hundred pounds and measure six feet fin to whisker.

A woman from Kitzmiller claimed to have seen Walter in the very Potomac that fed the river they were fishing. She said her husband wrestled Walter aboard their boat and yelled at her to go run and bring a camera. When she returned with the Polaroid, her husband was nowhere to be seen and Walter was flopping back into the water. Fifteen yards upriver, the fish spat out one of his shoes.

"Fine by me," said Durwood, who hadn't caught any trout. "Maybe the catfish'll change my luck."

Crole opened his tackle box. He took a finger of stink for himself, then offered the tin to Durwood.

After a moment, he said, "You alright, partner?"

Durwood was looking at the stink.

"I know you smelled it before," Crole said. "Now I did let the hog brains sit out an extra day, but—"

"That's not it," Durwood said.

Crole blew a breath through the gap in his teeth. He shaped the stink over his hook and casted.

Durwood did the same.

As they dragged their bait along the riverbed, Sue-Ann rolled from her left side over onto her right. Then back over left. She scratched behind her neck with her hind foot but couldn't reach whatever she was trying for. She kept scratching.

"Maybelle was a fine woman," Crole said. "But she's gone. Ain't coming back from the dead."

Durwood jerked his line, making an angry swirl in the water. "They oughta put you on daytime TV."

"You think?"

"I do. Give you a show. Microphone, studio audience."

Crole chuckled. "Me and Oprah."

Into the afternoon, Durwood's mood improved. Elk Garden helped. It felt like the lushest place on earth after Chickasaw, like the mountains and trees and sorghum stalks could trap time itself in their great number and slow its march.

The sun winked below the horizon near eight o'clock. Durwood bade Crole farewell and started for the house.

Through the line of cypress to the west, he saw a car approaching. Funny colored somehow. As it got closer, he made out a checked pattern of black and yellow.

Taxicab.

Not many taxicabs worked Elk Garden.

Durwood's heart jumped.

The taxicab turned into Durwood's property and motored toward the house. Its driver was easily identified by his shock of orange hair: Bucephelus T. Taggart. Buce had a different hustle every week. Durwood could still remember him selling pet rocks in school. According to scuttlebutt, his latest quest was to "introduce the gig economy" to Elk Garden.

The passenger was Carol Bridges.

Durwood covered ten yards in a blink to get her door.

She stepped from the car with a straight mouth.

"You ran off," she said.

Her mouth remained straight.

"Guess I did," Durwood said.

Carol Bridges looked around the farm, its beauty reflected in her brown eyes. When the eyes came back to Durwood, they sparked.

"You forgot your keys," she said.

Durwood squinted beyond the shed to where the Vanagon was parked. "Don't believe so."

"Not those," she said. "Your keys to the city."

Durwood took a second catching her meaning. Then he relaxed.

"Chickasaw has keys? The big gold ones?" He held his calloused hands a foot apart.

She took a step closer. "Ours are plastic."

"Plastic keys. Mm." He shook his head wistfully. "I should've stayed."

"You should have," she agreed.

But her mouth wasn't straight now. It was smiling.

They kissed. Durwood would've sworn her lips tasted even sweeter in West Virginia. He felt Taggert's hood cutting into the back of his thighs as Carol Bridges pressed forward. Their mouths traded initiative—she'd probe deeper, then his would cover hers, then back.

Several minutes in, with Durwood safely off his car, Bucephelus T. Taggart restarted his cab and drove off.

"I didn't bring much," Carol Bridges picked a duffel bag

off the gravel. "Toiletries and a change of clothes is about it."

"We got stores," Durwood said.

He took her bag, and they walked to the house. Sue-Ann came loping off the porch to sniff hello.

"There you are!" the mayor said, rubbing Sue's chin. "I have Deputy Gomez watching my German shepherd, Ace. I should've brought him."

Sue-Ann panted with pleasure.

Durwood's chest filled. Though he planted nothing he couldn't eat himself or sell to Nethkins Feed & Fertilizer, wildflowers sometimes did pop up in the yard. Now he noticed white mayapple, five-petaled purple geranium, even a jack-in-the-pulpit by the wheelbarrow. Sun and rain were all they'd needed.

He had one boot on the porch steps when he heard a distinct call—sharp first, then withering. Next came the drumming.

Durwood froze. He looked up.

Moving up the red maple, stopping at regular intervals to drill, was the yellow-bellied sapsucker. He had his eye on the squirrel nest.

"Excuse me," Durwood said, letting go of Carol Bridges's hand.

He reached around the doorjamb for the slingshot he'd made for just this chance, out of two cattle ribs and the high-tensile rubber Yakov—the arms dealer—had packed Durwood's last shipment of grenades in.

"Durwood..." The mayor crossed her arms over her chest. "What are you up to?"

He said quietly, "I'm setting a thing right," and tiptoed back into the yard until the sapsucker was in his sights.

Carol Bridges looked at Sue-Ann. The dog yawned.

Durwood found a large gravel pea, nestled it in the slingshot's rubber crotch, and pulled it back between the cattle ribs. He closed one eye.

The sapsucker moved in jukey hops, sideways, diagonal. His pecks sent good wood falling to the ground as sawdust. The foliage was too dense where the creature stood now for a clean shot.

Durwood moved to improve the angle.

"Durwood. Oak. Jones," he heard behind him.

Finally, the sapsucker reached the nest. The little devil took two skitters around the edge like some Mountaineers receiver celebrating in the end zone. He pulled a twig from the structure and dropped it over the side. Then he did more happy skittering, which cleared him of the foliage.

His beady eyes fixed on another twig—a twig those squirrels had carried a hundred feet into the sky to make a home in this peaceful tree.

Durwood released his pea of gravel. That was all she wrote for the thieving sapsucker.

Keep reading for a sneak peek at book three
in the Third Chance Enterprises saga,
featuring Molly McGill:

THE BEGONIA KILLER

THE BEGONIA KILLER

Sneak Peek

After twenty minutes on Martha Dodson's couch, listening to her suspicions about the neighbor three doors down, I respected the woman. She was no idle snoop. She'd noticed his compulsive begonia care out the window while making lavender sachets from burlap scraps. She hadn't even been aware of the papered-over bedroom above his garage until her postal carrier had commented.

I asked, "And the day he removed the begonias, how did you happen to see that?"

Martha set tea before me on a coaster, twisting the cup so its handle faced me. "Ziggy and I were out for a walk— he'd just done his business. I stood up to knot the bag..." Her kindly face curdled, and I thought she might be remembering the product of Ziggy's "business" until she finished, "Then we saw him start *hacking,* and scowling, and *thrusting* those clippers at his flowers."

Her eyes, a pleasing hazel shade, darkened at the memory. She added, "At his own flowers."

I gave her a moment. "The begonias were in a mailbox planter?"

"Right by the street, yes. The whole incident happened just a few feet from passing cars, from the sidewalk where parents push babies in strollers."

"Did he dispose of the mess afterward?"

"Immediately," Martha said. "He looked at his clippers for a second—the blades were streaked with green from all those leaves and stems he'd destroyed—then kind of recovered. He picked up everything and placed it in the yard-waste bin. Every last petal."

"He sounds meticulous."

"Extremely."

I jotted *Cleaned up begonia mess* in my notebook.

Maybe because of my psychology background—I'm twelve credit hours shy of a PhD—I like to start these introductory interviews by allowing clients time to just talk, open-ended. I want to know what *they* feel is important. Often this tells as much about them as it does about whatever they're asking me to investigate.

Martha Dodson had talked about children first. Her own, then mine. How many did I have? Where did they go to school? Only after these preliminaries were established did she tell me about the case itself, laying out the various oddities of her neighbor Kent Kirkland.

I was still waiting to hear the crux of her problem, the reason she wanted to hire McGill Investigators. (Full disclosure: Although the name is plural, there's only one investigator. Me.)

"That sounds like an intense, visceral moment," I said, squaring myself to Martha on the couch. "So has he...done something to your flowers? Are you engaged in a dispute with him?"

Martha shook her head. Then, with perfect composure, she said, "I think he's keeping a boy in the bedroom over his garage."

I felt like somebody had blasted jets of freezing air into both my ears. The pen I'd been taking notes with tumbled from my hand to the carpet.

"Wait, *keeping* a boy?" I said.

"Yes."

"Against his will? As in, kidnapping?"

Martha nodded.

I was having trouble reconciling this woman in front of me—cardigan sweater, hair in a layered crop—with the accusation she'd just uttered. We were sitting in a nice New Jersey neighborhood. Nicer than mine. We were drinking tea.

She said, "There might be two."

Now my notebook nearly dropped to the carpet.

"*Two?*" I said. "You think this man is holding *two* boys hostage?"

"I don't know for sure," she said. "If I knew for sure, I'd be over there breaking down the door myself. But I suspect it."

She explained that a boy had gone missing from the next town over. It'd been about a month ago—I vaguely recalled the news stories. The parents had been quoted as saying they had "lost track of" their son. They hadn't reported his disappearance until seventeen hours after last sighting him.

There were about a million dots to be connected from this case—which had briefly been national news, if I remembered right—to Kent Kirkland.

I left these dots aside for now. "How do you get to two?"

"There was another missing case, another boy. Eighteen months ago." Martha's mouth moved in place like she was counting up how many jars of tomatoes she'd canned last fall. "He lived close too. That case was complicated because the parents had just divorced, and the dad—who was a native Venezuelan—had just moved back. People suspected him of taking the kid with him."

"To Venezuela?"

"Yes. Apparently, the State Department couldn't get any answers."

I nodded—not because I accepted all that she was telling me but because there was no other polite response available.

Neither of us spoke. Together, our eyes drifted down the street to Kent Kirkland's two-story saltbox home. Pale-yellow vinyl siding. Chain-link fence. Three separate posted notices to *Please pick up after your pet*. A *Neighborhood Watch* sign at the corner.

Finally, I said, "Look, Mrs. Dodson. Martha. Most of the cases we handle at McGill Investigators are domestic in nature. Straying husbands. Teenagers mixed up with the wrong crowd. I'm a mother myself, and I've been a wife. Twice." I softened this disclosure with a smirk. "I generally take cases where my own life experiences can be brought to bear."

"But that's why I chose you." Martha worried her hands in her lap. "The ad said, 'Your case will be treated with dignity and discretion.' That's all I ask."

I looked into her eyes. "Okay."

She seemed to sense my reluctance and started, rushing,

"Those bedroom windows are papered over *twenty-four hours a day*! You didn't *see* him destroy those begonias. I did! I saw how he severed their stalks and shredded their root systems. You don't do that to flowers you've tended for an entire season. Not if you're a person of sound mind."

"Gardening is more challenging for some than others. I love rhododendrons, but I can't keep them alive. I overwater, I underwater. I plant them in the wrong spot."

"Have you ever massacred them in a fit of rage?"

"No." I smiled. "But I've wanted to."

Martha matched my smile, her eyes back on Kent Kirkland's house.

I said, "Some men aren't blessed with impulse control. Maybe he was a lousy gardener, he'd tried fertilizing and everything else, and these things just refused to—"

"But he *wasn't* a lousy gardener. He was excellent. I think he grew those begonias from seed. You know, they're supposed to be annuals here—we're in zone seven. They're supposed to die off in winter. But he wanted his to be perennials, to live on year after year."

Again, I was at a loss. I liked Martha Dodson. She had seemed like a reasonable person—right up until she'd started talking about kidnappings and Venezuela.

She scooted closer to me on the couch. "You didn't see the rage, Ms. McGill. I saw it. I saw him that day. He walked out of the garage with hand pruners, but he took one look at those begonias—leaves browning at the edges, those tangled stems like green worms—and he flipped out. Turned right around, put away the hand pruners, and came back with the clippers."

She mimed viciously snapping a pair of clippers closed.

"Rage is one thing," I said. "Kidnapping is another."

"Of course," Martha said. "That's why I'd like to hire you: to figure out what he might be capable of."

Her pupils seemed to pulse in place.

"I want to help you out, honestly." I took her hand. "I do. But this case feels outside my expertise."

"Is it the danger? Do you not handle dangerous jobs?"

I balked. In fact, I'd done extremely dangerous jobs before—but only as part of Third Chance Enterprises, the freelance small-force, private arms team led by Quaid Rafferty and Durwood Oak Jones.

We'd stopped an art heist in Italy. We'd saved the world from anarchist hackers. Sometimes I can hardly believe our missions happened. They feel like half dream, half 4D IMAX movies starring me. They only come along every couple years; just about the time I've started believing they actually *are* dreams, Quaid shows up again on my front porch.

"I don't mind facing danger on a client's behalf," I said. "But McGill Investigators isn't meant to replace the proper authorities. If you believe Mr. Kirkland is involved in these disappearances, your first stop should be the police."

"Mm." Martha's face wilted—I couldn't help thinking of those begonias. "Actually, it was."

"You spoke with the police?"

She nodded. "Yes. Well, more of a front-desk person. I told him exactly what I've been telling you today."

"How did he respond?"

There was a tapestry loom on the coffee table. Martha threaded her fingers through its empty spindles, seeming to need its feel.

"He said the department would 'give the tip its due

attention.' Then, on my way out, he asked if I'd ever read anything by J. D. Robb."

"The mystery writer?" I asked.

"Right. He told me J. D. Robb was really Nora Roberts, the romance novelist. He said I should try them. He had a hunch I'd like them."

My teeth were grinding.

I said, "Some men are idiots."

Martha's face eased gratefully. "Oh, my husband thinks the same. I'm a Yancy Park housewife with too much time on her hands. He says Kirkland's just an odd duck. When I told him about the begonias, he got this confused expression and said, 'What's a perennial?'"

I could relate. My first husband had once handed me baking soda when I'd asked for cornstarch to thicken up an Italian beef sauce. The dish came out tasting like soap. After I tracked down the mistake, he grumbled, "Ah, relax. They're both white powders."

As much as I probably should have, I couldn't tell Martha no. Not after this conversation.

"I suppose I can do some poking around," I said. "See if he, I dunno, buys suspicious items at the grocery store. Or puts something in his garbage that might have come from a child."

Martha lurched forward and squeezed my hands like I'd just solved the case of Jack the Ripper.

"That would be amazing!" she cried. "Thank you *so* much! I know this seems far-fetched, but my instincts tell me something's wrong and if I didn't follow through, if it turned out I was right and those little boys..."

She didn't finish. I was glad.